Irene Hughey

D0070531

THE LINK
And The
PROMISE

VIRGINIA HAVENS

Internation Standard Book Number
0-88290-211-3

Library of Congress Catalog Card Number
83-80407

Horizon Publishers Catalog and Order Number
1951

Printed and Distributed in the
United States of America
by

**Horizon
Publishers &
Distributors Inc.**

———————

**50 South 500 West
P.O. Box 490
Bountiful, Utah 84010**

*Jacket and cover photography and design by
Richard Jamison.*

TO MY MOTHER
Who believed in my right
to choose.

INTRODUCTION

There is a tie that links us inevitably with the past. The drama of our lives is played out on a stage that includes all mankind, both living and dead. Each touches and profoundly affects the other. The present generation is molded by the past, and past generations are reaching out to the present. It is incumbent upon us all to find that link in our own lives.

This is a story of two generations of a family over a hundred years and five generations apart, and of the link and the promise that drew them eternally together.

Chapter One

A pebble tossed in a stream barely disturbs the surface before it settles quietly on the bottom. But that pebble could, in time, become the catalyst that changes the course of the stream. So it is with a human life. A small, unimportant incident can change the course of that life, many lives, forever.

For Kaye Button, woman on her way up, her pebble was a dropped book in an elevator in the Hamilton Tower office building in St. Louis, Missouri, on a Monday at 8:20 a.m. The book was an index to the archives of Monroe County, Ohio. Yet the book was less the catalyst for change than was the young woman who dropped it.

She was about 21, pretty, with short, dark hair. Her eyes, too, were dark but her complexion was fair. At the moment, she seemed to be pre-occupied with what may have been the dullest book in the world; a book suddenly dumped onto the floor by a little man who wore owlish glasses and carried an oversized briefcase. Briefcase and book collided when he attempted to remove his hat with the hand that held the case instead of with his empty hand.

The book fell at Kaye's feet. She retrieved it. The little man blurted apologies, but before the girl could speak, the elevator door opened and he hurried away.

The two women laughed. "What a way to start a Monday," Kaye observed as she returned the book to its owner.

"Yes," said the girl, taking the book. The elevator door opened again, and the girl stepped out.

Kaye quickly dismissed the incident. Reaching the penthouse offices of the Hamilton Company, she hurried in. Wade would soon be there, and she wanted his work ready. Wade. Dear, kind, handsome Wade—and he loved her, too. How, she wondered, could she be blessed with so much! The world was in her hand. Kaye Button. Well-born, well-educated, she had first met Clayton Wade Hamilton III after graduation from the university when she

9

took a job at the Hamilton Importing Company. He was a member of his father's firm, destined some day to head it, and she, as an employee, was responsible directly to Wade.

For two years they had worked together. Now he was a junior partner, and she was more an administrative assistant than an executive secretary. He was elected a senator in Missouri's General Assembly, and a seat in the U.S. Senate was a definite possibility for his future.

Kaye was twenty-four, a trim five feet, six inches tall. Her almost shoulder-length blonde hair she sometimes wore in a high sophisticated style, and sometimes falling loose with short bangs brushed to the side. But always one was drawn to sensitive, intelligent blue eyes. She dressed with particular good taste, always looked like a woman who knew where she was going.

As for Wade, Kaye was first attracted to him by his handsome face— dark hair, hazel eyes, skin tanned from hours spent playing tennis. He was a strong man both physically and intellectually. Kaye was proud to realize that Wade set high goals and that he would undoubtedly reach them. She was pleased, perhaps flattered, that such a man would be interested in her! And always Wade treated her in a manner that showed he respected her intelligence, as well, giving her increased administrative responsibilities in the office.

Wade had a sweet, tender side to his nature, too, Kaye discovered. As they began to date, he was attentive, generous, and loving, and when he asked her to marry him, Kaye knew there was only one answer to give.

What more could she ask than this? Kaye thought. Together we can climb the heights. Nothing can stop us.

Kaye's office was a handsome room, decorated in blue with accents of glass, bronze and walnut. Wade's adjoining office was done in rich brown. Kaye sat at the walnut desk and pulled a legal document from her briefcase. The Missouri General Assembly was nearing the end of its session, and two of Wade's bills, with their amendments, were coming up for final action, possibly today. He would be flying to Jefferson City and the state's capitol building about 9 a.m. after being home for the weekend. The document Kaye held was the contract for a new line of merchandise from a plant in Hong Kong. The Hamilton Company was negotiating with it and needed Wade's review and signature before he left.

She set things in order at his desk and was busy at her own when Wade walked in at 8:30.

"Hi, my love," he greeted her with a kiss. "You're here early."

"Well, I knew you needed the Hong Kong contract in its final form before you leave for the capitol. I pulled the final strings together for you on Friday and had one of the secretaries type the document. Now you won't have to worry about it while you're gone."

"Thanks. I don't know what I'd do without you."

"Once this assembly session is over and the Hong Kong business is taken care of, you can marry me, and then you'll never be without me."

"Is that a threat or a promise?"

"A promise to love, honor and cherish if you do," she laughed, "and a threat to do you in if you don't."

"Can't wait to take you up on it," and he gave her cheek a peck as he went into his office.

The morning passed quickly. After Wade took care of matters which required his attention, he left. Kaye was so involved in her work that she hardly noticed the passage of time until she realized that she was hungry. She decided on a quick lunch in the building's cafeteria and went downstairs. She often had lunch with Wade out of the building, and she missed him.

In the cafeteria Kaye saw the dark-haired girl she had shared an elevator with earlier. She sat alone, her head buried in a book. The same book? Kaye walked over and tried to see the title. Sure enough, it was an index to the archives of Monroe County, Ohio. That was too much. Kaye had to know what was so fascinating.

Kaye was inquisitive by nature. For example, her curiosity had gotten her tongue stuck to a metal gatepost one January when she was a small child. She spent a night lost in the Canadian wilds during a family outing in her pre-teen years because she set out on her own to investigate something. In high school, her unauthorized experiments in chemistry brought her the assignment of an extra report, but the quality of the report eventually resulted in a college scholarship.

"May I share your table?" Kaye asked.

The girl looked up. "What? Oh, sure. Glad to have you." She gave a friendly smile as Kaye took a seat opposite her.

"I'm Kaye Button. I work upstairs."

"I'm Janice Connors. Call me Jan. I work here, too."

"What is that book? I noticed the title this morning in the elevator. What on earth is so fascinating about an index to an archives?"

"I'm trying to locate some of my ancestors who lived in Ohio," Jan explained, "and this index tells what records are available for searching. You know, marriage records, land grants, tax and probate records."

Kaye's face took on an amused look, which apparently did not escape Jan. "Genealogy may sound dull," Jan said, "but you'd be surprised how looking for your roots gets hold of you—sort of like being a Sherlock Holmes."

"If you say so," Kaye responded.

"No kidding!" Jan closed the book. "How much do you know about your heritage? Do you know anyone beyond your grandparents?"

"I must admit you've got me there. I don't know much. In fact, almost nothing."

"It could be interesting to find out."

Kaye was silent, thoughtful. "I do have a great-grandfather who was reared by a foster family."

"What happened to his own family?"

"I don't know. I know only that a family named Cook took him in until he was old enough to be on his own."

"That could be an interesting story. Just think! Your great-grandfather could have been stolen by Indians, then rescued by the cavalry and given to the—Cooks, did you say?" They both laughed.

"What an imagination you have," said Kaye. "I doubt whether anything as exciting and dramatic as that happened."

Jan glanced at her watch. "I have to get back. If you do find out anything exciting, let me know. I'm with Kenner & Blackmer, upstairs." She picked up her book and left.

Kaye realized she hadn't touched her food. She ate, not really aware of what was on her plate. Her mind was on her conversation with Janice Connors. Genealogy? Ancestors? Such foolishness! Yet, what about Great-grandfather Button? What did happen? He wasn't stolen by Indians. Was he? Oh, did it really matter whether he was? Of course not!

She went back to her office, but her mind began to wander. Drawn suddenly back to reality, she saw that she had doodled a stick figure of an Indian. Vaguely embarrassed, she wadded the paper and threw it away.

At a meeting with the section heads, she studied various faces and imagined each with a feathered headdress passing a peacepipe over a treaty which concerned a white baby in a papoose cradle. Kaye smothered a giggle.

That evening as Kaye and Wade were dining at their favorite restaurant, she thought again of her conversation with Jan.

"How much do you know about your ancestors?" she asked Wade.

"What's the matter?" he responded, smiling. "Afraid there's a skeleton in my closet? Getting cold feet about marrying me?"

"Of course not, honey," she replied. "I just had a conversation today with a girl who is looking into her background, and I've been thinking since about mine. Tell me, what do you know? A lot—or just a little, like me?"

"Practically nothing," Wade laughed. "That's one of the reasons I love you, Kaye. You come up with the most unexpected ideas."

"Well?" she asked after the waiter who served their dinners had left.

"Well, what?"

"What do you know about your ancestors?"

"I believe there's a family tradition that the Hamiltons are descended from someone who came over on the Mayflower. But I don't really know. Why does it matter?"

"I don't know that it does. But Jan did start me wondering what I really do know about my heritage."

"Kaye, sweetie, don't lose any sleep over it. Your heritage doesn't matter to me. You can share my Mayflower blueblood. Now eat. I have to go back to Jeff City tonight."

Lying in her dark bedroom Kaye did think again about her heritage. Finally, she got up and turned on the light. She sat down and wrote a letter to her father asking him what he knew about his grandfather. Where did he come from? Why was he reared by a foster family? What happened to his parents? What were their names? When she could think of no more questions to ask, Kaye put the letter with her purse to be mailed in the morning, and went back to bed.

She remembered Wade's question: "Why does it matter?" The situation was curious. Why should she be so suddenly taken with the idea of knowing her heritage? Maybe, if she should see Jan Connors again, she'd ask why Jan found genealogy so interesting and important.

Chapter Two

By the time the letter from her father reached Kaye, she had nearly forgotten the incident with Jan. She had not seen Jan in the elevator nor had she eaten in the building cafeteria since their initial meeting.

Kaye tore open the letter and read:

"I know little about my Grandfather Button's background. As you know, he was reared by this family named Cook. I think he said something about coming from somewhere in Pennsylvania with them. I believe they came by boat down the river to Marietta, or wherever it was that they settled. He was only a baby at the time. When he was 16 or 17, he went on down the river to Cincinnati to make his mark on the world. You know the rest.

"I don't know his parents' names nor what happened to them. I'm sorry I can't tell you any more. The family long ago lost contact with any of those Cooks, so I can't even refer you to anyone there who might know. I don't think that anyone in our family knows more than that either.

"What's the sudden interest? Why does it matter? . . ."

Kaye dropped the letter in her lap. She was disappointed that there was so little information.

Ohio, she thought. That's where Jan was looking for information. I wonder if she could tell me where to look for my ancestors. She glanced at the letter again. Dad's question was the same as Wade's—"Why does it matter?" Maybe Jan can answer that one, too, Kaye thought.

Next day was the final day of the General Assembly. Wade was tied up at the capitol since the session would not adjourn until midnight.

That means I'll be free for lunch. I wonder if Jan will be, she thought. I'll call her and see. Where was it she said she worked? Kenner and . . . hmmm.

Kaye hurried to the cafeteria and picked out a quiet table where they could talk. In moments Jan appeared.

"Hi! What's up? What's the news you have?" Jan asked.

"Not as much as I had hoped for but . . ." Kaye showed Jan her father's letter. "Where do I go from here? You were looking for records in Ohio. Would there be anything there to help me locate my Great-grandfather Button?"

Jan looked thoughtful. "Yes, we should be able to find information in both the city library and the branch library—census records, tax lists. Do you know whether they were land owners or what church they belonged to? That could help us, too."

"Would you help me?" Kaye asked, "I don't know where to start."

"Sure. I'd love to. Would you, by any chance, be free tonight?"

Kaye hesitated for a moment. Wade would be at the capitol in Jefferson City until the General Assembly adjourned tonight, and he wouldn't fly home until morning. Perhaps she'd better take this opportunity to go with Jan.

"Yes, I think I can," she replied. She told Jan about Wade and his work in the assembly and also of their plans to marry in the near future.

Jan smiled. "I'm getting married soon myself!" she said. "His name is Jimmy Halvorsen." Glancing at her watch she exclaimed "Where has the time gone? I must get back. Can you meet me at this address about six tonight?" On a piece of paper she wrote an address unfamiliar to Kaye.

"I think I can make it," Kaye responded.

"The library is open until ten but I think you'll find you can use that much time. It passes so quickly there."

Kaye shrugged. Time passes fast in a library? she thought, but agreed, and they walked to the elevator together.

That night Kaye drove to the address Jan had given her, but she could see nothing that looked like a library. She was in a residential neighborhood and the address appeared to be that of a church building.

"The Church of Jesus Christ of Latter-day Saints," she read on the bronze tablet on the side of the building. She was not sure she'd ever heard of such a church before.

Just then Jan appeared from around the corner of the building.

"Hi!" she called. "You're right on time!"

"Hi, there. I thought we were going to a library, and here we are at a church."

Jan laughed. "I'm sorry. I should have explained. This is the branch library of the big genealogy library in Salt Lake City. It's in the back of the building."

They walked around to the side of the building, entered and went down a stairway. In a big room were shelves of books, files of microfilms, perhaps half a dozen microfilm readers, and copying machines. Most of all, Kaye noticed the warm, comfortable atmosphere and the friendliness of the people as they worked.

"From what you've told me," said Jan, "the Cook family might have been in Marietta, Ohio, in 1870, so we might be able to locate them in the 1870 census." Jan went to select a microfilm and they found a reader. "This is the census for Washingon County, where Marietta is. Look for a family named Cook coming from Pennsylvania and with a child in the family with the last name of Button. I'll be right here working on my own things.''

Kaye began turning the film, hoping that the Cook family would show up on the first page, then the second, the third . . . She continued to search until the last page of the Marietta census had passed.

"Jan," she whispered, "they're not in Marietta."

"Well, then, they might be in the township or somewhere else in the county. Just keep looking," and Jan flashed a smile.

Kaye continued to search. She glanced at the clock on the wall. Jan was right about the time. She was amazed at how fast the hours had gone by. She looked around the room to see what was going on and to give her eyes a rest from the film. Trying to read sometimes nearly unreadable handwriting, alternating between hope and disappointment as she slowly turned the pages, was turning out to be a strain.

She was nearly to the end of the film, so she sighed and turned back to finish it up. Her sigh turned to a gasp. There it was! It bounced out of the page at her as though to say, "Here we are!"

Kaye read the entry carefully: Oliver Cook, age 35, born Pennsylvania, father and mother born Pennsylvania; Mollie, age 33, she and her parents also born in Pennsylvania; Oliver Junior, 10, Henry, 8, Betsy, 6, with the same Pennsylvania notations; David, 4, Annabelle, 2, born in Ohio. Last on the list, William A. Button, age 5, Pennsylvania notation for birth.

She grabbed Jan's arm. "Jan! Jan! Look! It's here!" They whispered excitedly over the entry.

"Of course," said Jan, "this doesn't give us William's parents or where in Pennsylvania they all came from, but it's a start. We know the Cooks' names now."

"Let's get started on the next step."

"This record says Oliver was a farmer. We could check land records. Or perhaps he left a will in which William was mentioned." They discussed several possibilities and determined that some correspondence to county court houses would be in order. From that basis they organized their next steps, hurrying because the library was closing.

As they walked out of the building, Kaye was both excited and thoughtful.

"Jan," she asked, "why does it matter? That's the question both Wade and my father asked about genealogy. I couldn't answer them. It is more than just curiosity, isn't it?"

"Well," said Jan, "as I'm sure you know by the church building here and the library, I'm a Mormon. For me, genealogy is tied up in my church, but if you'd like to know about it, I'd be glad to tell you."

"I'd never heard the name that was on the building, but when you mentioned Salt Lake City, I got the connection. I have heard of Mormons, but I don't know much about them.''

'' 'Mormon' is just a nickname.''

"What is genealogy to the Mormons?''

"I don't live far from here, Kaye. Let's go over to my place where we can talk for awhile.''

* * *

Jan's apartment, while not extravagant, was pleasant and comfortable. She showed Kaye a photo of her family, and told her a little about each person. Then she picked up a photo of a handsome young man. "This is Jimmy,'' she said fondly. "As soon as he gets his degree—electrical engineering, he's in computers—we'll be married in the Washington, D.C., Temple . . . just a couple of months from now.''

Kaye sat down on a comfortable sofa, and Jan brought cold milk and cake from the kitchen.

"Now, to answer your question,'' Jan began. "I guess my wedding is a good place to start.'' She put her glass of milk on the coffee table.

"Your wedding?'' Kaye was a bit surprised.

"Yes. You see, our marriage will not just be 'until death do you part' or 'as long as you both shall live.' Ours will be not only for this life but for all eternity.''

"That's asking a lot of a marriage, isn't it? Of course, if you are truly and deeply in love . . .'' Kaye's voice trailed off as she thought of Wade.

"Yes. What's the point of families if all ties are broken at death? Our Heavenly Father never intended that such ties should be broken. Your companion can always be your companion and your children are yours forever.''

"I like the idea of Wade and I always being together.''

"But the eternal marriage ceremony has to be performed by the people who have the authority or it is of no avail. I mean, our government wouldn't be obliged to accept naturalizations by people who had no authority to do that, would it?''

"All right, I think I see your point. They have to be authorized.''

"I won't go into the details of authority right now. That's a whole new ball game. Just keep in mind this one point. In Matthew in the New Testament, Christ gave the Apostle Peter the power to seal, or make binding, in Heaven those ordinances he, as an apostle, performed on earth.''

"Are you telling me that the binding power is what makes marriages and families go on forever? Is that what's behind your interest in doing family research?''

"Yes, you're right on target. Do you remember in the New Testament when Nicodemus went to the Savior at night and asked what he had to do to be saved?''

Kaye nodded, although her remembrance was vague.

Jan continued, her face alight with an enthusiasm Kaye had not seen her show before. "Christ told Nicodemus that he would have to be born again—born of the water and the spirit, or, in other words, baptized. Christ said that everyone would have to be born again, or baptized, and He made no exceptions. Does that put a question in your mind?"

Kaye studied the face of her new friend. She was obviously having a good time explaining her beliefs. Taking a bite of cake she had almost forgotten, Kaye considered her answer.

"There have been a lot of people on the earth that never even heard of Christianity. And, come to think of it, wasn't Jesus known only in a small part of the world in his time? You want me to ask what happens to the rest of those people, don't you?"

"You're right with me," Jan laughed.

"So? What does happen?"

"Well, the New Testament tells us that during the time that Christ's body lay in the tomb, before his resurrection, he was in the spirit world organizing missionary work for the people who lived at the time of Noah."

"I've never heard that before."

"It's there in black and white, and we are told why. And to carry the explanation a step further, the Apostle Paul talked to the members of the church in his time about doing baptisms for the dead."

Kaye shook her head. "I'm sorry, but aren't you getting just a little carried away?"

"Incredible?" Jan asked, then answered, "It's there. The members of that church in Corinth asked if there would really be a resurrection, and Paul answered by saying, in essence, 'Of course, there's a resurrection. Why are you doing baptisms for the dead if the dead rise not at all?' "

Kaye remained silent. This was all so—so unheard of.

"That's it in a nutshell. We search out our ancestors so that we can do their baptisms by proxy and so that they can be married and have their children sealed to them for eternity, also by proxy. That's why the temples. The people who have this authority to seal are there, and only there."

Subdued and thoughtful, and not convinced, Kaye spoke, "I've never heard of such ideas before."

"I don't suppose you have. Christ did a proxy work for us by paying for our sins if we repent and also by breaking the bonds of death so we will all be resurrected, something we could not do for ourselves. We have the blessed opportunity to do for our kindred dead something they are not able to do for themselves," Jan explained. Kaye's face was a picture of amazement. "Full circle," said Jan.

"And that's what's behind your genealogical research! But what if those people don't want this proxy work done for them—even supposing this is all true?"

"They always have their right to choose. Since we have no way of knowing whether they will accept our work for them, we just do the work and they can accept it or reject it."

"Fair enough."

"And, admittedly, much simplified, that's all there is to our beliefs concerning genealogy. We start with the known—us—and work our way back."

There was silence before Jan spoke again. "That's enough for tonight. I don't want to overdo this."

* * *

All the way home Kaye kept going over her conversation with Jan. She didn't know whether she believed what she had been told. Yet to have Wade for always—what a wonderful thought! What will Wade think? she wondered. And whether Jan was right or not, the curiosity that got Kaye into so many strange situations made her want to find that elusive Great-grandfather Button.

Remembering the Ohio county archives index that introduced her to Jan, Kaye laughed aloud. Now *she* was looking into those Ohio records!

Chapter Three

The late afternoon sun hung low in the sky. In an hour or two it would be down. It peeked through the trees as though to get one last glimpse of the land before dropping below the horizon. A twitter of birds could be heard as they began the last rounds of worm gathering before settling down their newly hatched broods for the coming night, and an owl, somewhat disgruntled at being awakened early for its night foraging, hooted and glided to a neighboring tree.

The owl, in turn, intruded on a large grey squirrel, which promptly gave forth with a noisy tongue-lashing. A wide-eyed deer stepped cautiously into a small clearing to see what all the noise was about.

Caroline Marchant was oblivious to the natural beauty around her as she urged her little horse, Silky, down the road. On such a beautiful spring day she had been happy for an excuse to leave her chores at the house and go into town. Her mother had letters to post to her brothers fighting with the Union forces in Virginia. Caroline had taken the opportunity to go over to the Cook farm for a visit with her good friend, Mollie, on her return.

Caroline and Mollie had been close friends ever since the Marchants had come to the Monongahela Valley of southwest Pennsylvania from Connecticut five years earlier, in 1858. Caroline was only fifteen then, and Mollie twenty, but there developed quickly a bond of greatest friendship. When, a year later, Mollie married the jovial Oliver Cook, Caroline was her attendant. She was the first, after Oliver, to know of the expected birth of young Oliver and later Henry. On this, little Henry's first birthday, Caroline was at the Cook farm until the afternoon was well spent.

She was anxious now to get home. It wasn't safe to be out in the woods after dark. Rumors were circulating that Confederate spies had been seen in the area. Only rumors, of course, and they had been flying everywhere lately. Sometimes the rumors were of civilian spies, other times military scouts or couriers, and still others of slaves escaping from the south due to President Lincoln's Emancipation Proclamation and the "underground

20

railway.'' Caroline pulled her shawl more tightly around her shoulders and prodded the horse again.

She could hear the gurgling of the creek a little below the level of the road, and let the pony take its lead down the bank for a drink. Silky stuck his muzzle into the clear, cold water. A raccoon wandered onto the scene to wash its meal and, startled by the unexpected company, scurried off. Caroline turned to watch it and, as she did, her shawl slipped from her shoulders and fell to the ground. She dismounted to retrieve it.

It was then she heard the sound. Hardly audible above the babbling of the stream, there came a soft, low moan. Caroline froze in her tracks, and under her breath she whispered, "Dear God, protect me.'' She strained to hear the sound again. She hoped that she really wouldn't, that it was just an overactive imagination. Then it came again—a moan, a soft sound escaping from the lips of someone apparently in pain. Caroline stood a moment longer, ready to get away fast. Then her compassion for someone in need of help overcame her fear of whatever or whoever it might be. She moved cautiously toward the bushes where the sound had come from and carefully pushed them aside. Lying partially hidden in the undergrowth near the stream, a man lay, unconscious.

Blood matted his light brown hair and ran down his pale face. Caroline knelt down and touched his forehead. It was hot. He was no one she had ever seen before and there appeared nothing about him that gave any clue as to who he was or where he came from.

Now what should I do? she wondered. It looks like he has a leg injury of some sort, but if it's broken I might just make it worse if I try to get him on my horse. He might be dangerous, but I can't just leave him here to die.

She turned him carefully onto his back and cushioned his head with her shawl. Rinsing her handkerchief in the stream, she wiped the blood from his face. She dipped the handkerchief again in the water and placed it folded on his forehead. Then she mounted Silky and hurried toward home, knowing she needed to get help as soon as possible.

Reaching the Marchant farm, Caroline started toward the house to find her father. But she stopped short as she heard voices coming from the front porch.

". . . but he got away, I guess,'' her father was saying.

"Are they sure he was a Rebel?'' asked her mother.

"Don't know if they're really sure about anything. Barney apparently saw him snooping around and figured he was up to no good. When he hollered, the man took off like a shot. And that's just what Barney did—shot.''

"Did he hit the man?''

"Barney said he thought he did. Maybe a couple of times. He took off on his horse and disappeared into the hills. It's been a couple of days, so he's either dead or long gone.''

"How does he know he hit the Reb?"

"The guy just acted like he'd been hit—jumped, you know—and there was a bit of blood on the ground, but they couldn't follow it. He must have fallen off his horse but got back on, and they couldn't even find his tracks."

"What do you suppose he was after?"

"Who knows? With the mining around this part of the state, and the river route to Pittsburgh, oh, it could be anything."

There was a pause, a deep sigh, and Mrs. Marchant said, "This awful war! Oh, James, when I think of our Johnny and Charles off in Virginia fighting . . . I hope they get that Reb and hang him!"

"Maude, I feel the same way. I'd shoot a Reb, too, and not wait to ask questions."

Caroline stayed concealed in the shadows. So that's who I found, she thought, that Rebel. Yet she could see in her mind the pale, young face. He could be one of her brothers lying wounded behind Confederate lines. Wouldn't she want someone to take care of him? Maybe she could just tend to his wounds and then turn him in. Obviously she couldn't tell her father now about finding him.

Caroline slipped into the house by the back door. Quickly she collected medications, cloths for bandages, a blanket and pillow from her bed, and slipped out again. Her mother and father were still on the porch. A plan was forming in her mind. She mounted Silky and was off.

At first she didn't see the man. He had dragged himself away from the creek and was lying hidden behind some bushes. Their eyes met, and for a moment neither spoke. He had one arm behind him, and she could see that he held a large stone ready to defend himself.

"I brought bandages. You look like you could use some help," she said.

He relaxed his grip on the stone. "Thank you. I really don't feel so good."

Caroline cleaned and bandaged the wound on his head. She had to hurry. The sun was now not far above the horizon, soon to drop out of sight behind the hills. The man was obviously unable to walk, but if she could get him on the horse, she could take him to an old shack not far from where they were. It has been built by early trappers and, being just within the Marchant property, had been used by them for various purposes.

She would take the Rebel there for the night, and decide what to do tomorrow. The shack was out of the way and not likely to be seen.

"You're a stranger here," she said. "At least, I've not seen you before."

"I'm just passing through."

"How did you get hurt? Horse throw you?" she asked, hoping to appear innocent. She could almost feel his eyes searching her face for any sign of what she might be thinking.

"Yes," he responded. "A snake startled him and he hooked me on a tree limb."

She didn't speak, so he continued.

"The horse ran off. I don't know where he is now. I assume it was you who found me earlier."

"Yes."

"Does anyone else know?"

"No. Why? Are you hiding from someone? The law?"

"I have broken no law. I have my own reasons."

"I'll respect that for the moment." Caroline stood up. "I'll take you to a place where you'll be safe for the night, that is, if you can get on my horse."

"I thank you for that."

Painfully, and with great effort, he rose to his feet. He was tall and well built, strong from time obviously spent outdoors. Supporting himself on Caroline's shoulder he grimaced as he mounted her horse. Then she mounted and they rode into the thick growth of trees and bushes that covered the hilly countryside.

Caroline nearly missed the old log hut, so well hidden in the trees. The hut contained a table, a bench, a bed with a straw tick, and a fireplace. She half supported, half dragged the injured man into the hut and to the bed where he collapsed. Caroline could see he was in pain and weak from loss of blood.

Twilight was deepening. Caroline knew she must hurry or her absence would bring on questions at home. She removed the injured man's boots, cut away the torn and bloody trouser leg and, as best she could, dressed the wound which was jagged and deep, likely a bullet wound. The bullet was probably still in, which would explain the fever, but she couldn't see to get it out now.

She put the pillow under his head, spread the blanket over him, and picked up her things. The man's eyes were closed, so she merely said she would be back in the morning, and went out to Silky.

Next morning, Caroline waited impatiently for her father to finish breakfast and be off to the fields. Her mother announced that she would be spending the day with a neighbor helping out, and Caroline gave a sigh of relief. She would be free now to go to the Rebel without having to fabricate a story. She disliked the deceit but she couldn't turn in a sick man possibly to be hanged. As soon as her parents were gone, she packed food for the man and collected other things she thought she might need, tied them on back of her saddle and left for the shack.

The Rebel lay there unconscious. The injured leg was badly inflamed, and his forehead still felt fevered. There was no doubt in Caroline's mind that this was the man Barney had shot. She had to get that bullet out of his leg. With fear and trepidation, she probed and, fortunately, was able to find and remove the bullet. She then cleaned the wound as best she could and dressed it.

Caroline brought cool water from the stream and bathed his face. Only then did she take time to look closely at the man she had rescued. He had several days' growth of beard on a face tanned by the sun. He looked the role of a Pennsylvania farmer, but his manner and words showed a gentility some of the rough-hewn people of that area lacked.

Caroline also wondered how anyone could be sure this man was a Confederate. His clothes were the same that everyone around wore— nothing at all to arouse suspicion. She checked his pockets but there was nothing of interest there, either.

Caroline wondered how long it would take the Rebel to recover enough that she would be able to turn him in. There appeared to be no broken bones, but the bullet had done sufficient damage to the thigh and had been there so long that, with the loss of blood and the fever, the wounded man would be in no condition to move for a few days. He might be weak from lack of food, too. Caroline kept wet cloths, cold from the stream, on his forehead.

*   *   *

In time, the fever broke. The Rebel slept and, after sleeping, awoke. When he opened his eyes, Caroline was the first thing he saw.

"Hello," he said.

"Hello, yourself," she responded with a smile. "I think we can safely say you will make it now."

He weakly returned her smile.

"Are you hungry?" she asked. "It's been awhile since you've eaten."

"Yes, and I'm terribly thirsty, too."

She brought him water, cradling his head in her arms to help him drink. He watched as she removed, from a basket, milk, bread and butter. As she moved about, Caroline did not seem to be aware of the attractive picture she made but the watching man thought she was quite possibly the loveliest thing he had ever seen. With blue eyes in a sweet face framed by long blonde hair, which had been pulled back and pinned, she looked too fragile to be a farm girl. Although she was a small person, she moved with ease and always seemed to have her next move organized. He wondered what she had in mind to do with him.

"You are the prettiest girl I've ever seen," he said, and Caroline's cheeks turned pink. "What's your name, angel from heaven?"

"Caroline. Caroline Marchant," she responded. "You haven't told me yours."

"No, I haven't."

She brought a bowl of bread and milk to him and propped him up. "You didn't get thrown from a horse," she said carefully, watching his reaction.

"I didn't?"

"I got a bullet out of your leg. Horses don't do that."

"My gun went off accidentally when my horse threw me?"

"You didn't have a gun." Caroline paused. "I know who shot you."

The Rebel looked up abruptly, then continued eating. "Tell me about it," he said.

"A neighbor took a couple of shots at you a few days ago. He thought you were a Confederate spy." She watched his face, but his deep blue eyes betrayed nothing. He seemed to look right into her thoughts.

"Do you think I'm a spy?"

"I think so," she said softly, looking at the floor, "or else a military scout."

"Then why didn't you turn me in," he asked, "or just let me die?"

Caroline gave a long sigh. When she looked up, her eyes were moist. "I hate this terrible war!" she explained. "Americans killing Americans. My oldest brother, William, was one of the first to join the Union forces when the war broke out. He was also one of the first to be killed. Now my other two brothers have joined up—Johnny and Charles. They are in Virginia right now. This whole thing has really affected my mother. She cries at the least little thing, and Father is so full of hate for the Rebs . . ." She shuddered.

Neither spoke for a moment, and then she continued.

"You're a Reb but you're an American. You didn't kill William but your army did. I could help you and then let you go free to kill my other brothers, or I could let you die alone in the wilds and see you in my mind every day for the rest of my life. I keep thinking that maybe someone would do for my brothers what I'm doing for you if they should need it."

Caroline stopped speaking, and sat fingering the blanket.

"You know I'm a Confederate," the Rebel finally said, "and that's about all I can tell you. You can understand that. But there are principles that must be defended, and homes. My father has a plantation, and it is so close to the fighting that my home and my family could be wiped out at any time." He sighed. "You are truly an angel, Caroline, for caring for me and protecting me. But what are you going to do now?"

"Right now I'm going home before I have to account for where I have been all day." Caroline rose and began to gather her things. "Don't try to leave. You're not well enough to get far in these hills. I give you my word that I'll not tell anyone about you—at least not yet. I'll be back tomorrow as soon as I can get away unseen. I'll bring food and change those bandages."

She paused in the doorway. Light from the setting sun glowed like a halo around her small form while the evening breeze softly played with her skirts.

"Please trust me," she said.

The Rebel watched her go. Perhaps, as little as he had said, he'd told her too much. She could go to the authorities and turn him in, or go to her father to have him killed. Perhaps he should try to get out now while there was still a little daylight, and travel as far as he could. But in his condition that wouldn't be far. The next person to find him might not be so kind. Somehow, he felt that he could trust the girl, at least for another day, when he would be stronger. He lay back on the bed and fell asleep.

* * *

Outside, Caroline tied her basket to the back of Silky's saddle, mounted, and let the horse pick a path down the rough, overgrown creekside trail to the main creek and the road toward home.

I must try to see Mollie to ask her what she thinks should be done about the Rebel, Caroline thought. Mollie can help me think through this problem. She can help me to decide on the best course of action. Maybe I can get there tomorrow after I've been to the shack. But William, Johnny and Charles notwithstanding, Caroline knew in her heart that she could never turn the Rebel in.

Chapter Four

Bright sun streaming in her bedroom window woke Caroline. She could hear birds singing outside and her mother downstairs fixing breakfast. The smell of bacon and flapjacks tickled her nose. She thought of the Rebel down in the shack and wished that she could take him some. But she couldn't even cook for him there. Smoke from a fire would surely give his presence away. How much longer, she wondered, could she keep the Rebel hidden? How long before he would be strong enough to be able to slip away?

And one more thing, how much longer would she be able to find excuses to leave the house without having to answer questions. What reason could she think of today? Caroline dressed and went downstairs, anxious to know whether there was still talk of the Rebel among the townsfolk.

"Good morning, dear," her mother greeted her.

"Good morning, Mother. That sure smells good."

"Get some of these flapjacks while they're nice and hot. Those on that plate—I just took them out of the pan."

Caroline took the cakes, buttered them, added rich maple syrup, put two slices of thick bacon on her plate as well, then poured a glass of milk.

"Mother, I heard something about a Reb in the area the other day. Do you know anything about it?"

"Barney caught one in town where he shouldn't be, I guess. Don't know just where. He ran outside to his horse. Barney shot at him, but he still got away. That was the day your father was out of town, so he didn't learn of it until yesterday."

"Are they sure the man was a Reb?"

"They found his horse and gun, and there were maps and things in his saddle bag."

"Do they know who he was? Was there anything with his name on it?"

"Caroline, you're asking a lot of questions!"

"I'm just curious."

Mrs. Marchant filled a dishpan with hot water from the stove's reservoir and began washing dishes. Then she continued, "I believe your father said there was a name but I don't know what it was. The Rebs are all nameless, faceless demons to me."

Caroline finished her breakfast while her mother continued. "They don't know what happened to him, but I understand he didn't have a chance to get anything important. Thank the Lord for that. When I think what the Rebs did to my boy . . ." She began to weep softly.

Caroline rose and put her arm around her mother. "One day," she said, "this horrible war will be over. Then we can forgive and forget."

There was bitterness in the older woman's voice. "I can never forgive them for killing my William! Never!"

"They're our countrymen, Mother."

"I can never forgive them! And don't you talk that way! They're Rebels, killing our boys and fighting our government!"

"Are they still looking for that man?"

"I don't know. It would be pretty hard to find him in these mountains. Most likely wild animals have gotten him," and she added under her breath, "I hope."

"I'm sorry my questions upset you, Mother."

"I'm not upset!" Maude Marchant slammed a pan onto the stove and kicked the cabinet door closed.

Caroline said, "Unless you have something in particular you want me to do today, I'm going over to Mollie's for awhile. I promised to give her the pattern for Grandmother's wedding-ring quilt. This looks like a beautiful day for a ride."

"That's up to you. The garden needs weeding, though."

"There'll be time when I get back."

"Well, go and enjoy your day." Maude picked up an egg basket and went out to the chicken house.

Caroline went upstairs for the quilt pattern and to get a change of clothes from her brothers' things for the Rebel. Then she packed a basket of food, mounted Silky and rode off.

When she reached the shack, Caroline found the Rebel watching from the window.

"You're certainly looking better," she said as she prepared thick slices of bread and butter, meat and cheese, and a dish of strawberries from the garden.

"I feel much better. You can't believe how good that looks. I'm starved!"

While he ate, Caroline probed for more information.

"I learned this morning," she said, "that your horse was found . . ." She watched his eyes for a reaction but there was none. ". . . complete with saddle bag."

He looked up but continued to eat. "Not much could be learned from what was there," he replied.

"Your name was there."

"So, now my name is no secret."

"No, I still don't know your name. My mother—I didn't tell her about you—she couldn't remember it. Surely there's nothing now to stop you from telling me."

"I suppose not. My name's Alex—Alexander Cameron."

"How do you do, Alexander Cameron," she said, mockingly solemn.

"Glad to meet you, Caroline Marchant," he echoed her.

The situation suddenly seemed so ludicrous that they both burst out laughing. With their laughter, the tension eased. The mutual feeling of uncertainty and distrust melted away. For a little while the war ceased to exist. They were simply two young people chatting together on a fine late spring morning. A squirrel darted through the open door and, seeing he was not alone, gave a twitch of his tail and scurried out.

Alex smiled. "I used to chase squirrels when I was a youngster," he said. "Had the greatest dog. We spent a lot of good times together."

"Where's home?"

"Virginia. Not far from Richmond. My ancestors settled there a hundred and fifty years ago and built up a plantation. After my father dies, the place will belong to my brother and me."

"A real plantation? A big, beautiful mansion with columns in front?"

"Let's just say it's not too bad." He added, "We raise mostly cotton."

"You also have slaves, I guess." Caroline lowered her eyes disclosing her disapproval.

"Don't you see, the whole economy of the South is dependent on cotton, and machines can't handle the job of producing it. To me, the owning of slaves is . . . well, an unpleasant necessity."

"To buy and sell people just isn't right."

Alex sighed. "Caroline, I was raised in that situation. We've had our slaves for many years and they've never been abused. Mammy Rose was my nurse, and her boy, Luke, was my best friend."

"But still they weren't free," Caroline responded.

"I've been in the North and seen the industrialization going on. You don't find that in the Confederate states. Cotton is our life. Machines can't pick it. Oh, I'd like to free our slaves and maybe someday we can, when a machine can pick cotton."

"I guess I can understand how you feel," she said with a frown, "but I can't agree with it. When the war is over, the slaves will be free. President Lincoln has already issued the proclamation."

"The Confederacy will have second thoughts about that," Alex said grimly.

"But the Confederacy wants to divide the country."

"We were a group of sovereign states banded together in a common interest. The federal government wanted to take away from us rights that belonged to those states."

"Yes, to the states, not little independent countries. We're a union. If we don't stick together, our nation will surely be destroyed."

"I see what you're saying, too."

For a moment, neither spoke. Alex shifted his position and grimaced in pain. "This is a subject we could discuss for hours, but frankly it's too much for me right now. Later?"

"Of course. But, all in all, I'm glad I met you." She held out her hand.

Alex smiled and took her hand in his. "I'm glad you did, too. Otherwise I might be dead. You've been very good to me and I'm grateful."

Noting the time, Caroline decided she'd better be on her way. "If you don't mind my saying so, Mr. Cameron, you need a bath. I've brought you some of my brothers' clothes, and I'll bring water from the creek."

"I get deeper and deeper in your debt. But I'll repay you some day."

"I told my mother I was going to visit my friend, Mollie Cook. She and her husband, Oliver, have a farm not far from here. I'll check in here on my way home."

She put the remainder of the food she had brought on the bench where she had been sitting and hurried out the door calling, "See you later, Alex."

* * *

Mollie listened quietly as Caroline told her friend of Alex. She had heard of the encounter with the Confederate spy in town earlier, "But never did I expect you to be harboring him!" she exclaimed.

"Have I done something terrible—like treason?" asked Caroline fearfully.

"Oh, I hardly think anything like that. At least, your motives were honorable." Little Henry had pulled out all the contents of a cabinet that were within his reach. Mollie handed him a toy and put the rest of the things back. "I rather think I'd do the same thing. I couldn't let anyone just lie and suffer, either."

"I don't know how long I can keep him hidden nor how long before he'll be able to go. He seems to be getting his strength back quickly—faster than I had expected. I don't dare tell Mother or Father. They are so bitter."

You rather like the man, don't you? Is he handsome?"

Caroline considered the question while Mollie retrieved Henry. He had pulled himself up on a chair by the table and was churning with a chubby fist a pan of milk ready to be taken to the ice house for the cream to rise and be skimmed. She washed the little hand and again gave him his own toys.

"Handsome?" Caroline echoed. "It's hard to tell. He has several days' shaggy growth of beard. But, yes, I think he would be. I guess I am rather taken by him. He's kind and gentle, but strong and rugged."

Three-year-old Ollie came in carrying a cat that seemed resigned to whatever fate it might be facing. Henry immediately decided on his next conquest, and the poor cat found itself in the midst of a tug-of-war. Mollie extricated the animal, and put both boys down for naps.

"What are you going to do about the Rebel?" she asked.

"I simply can't turn him in now. Yet I have no idea what his mission was and whether he really is dangerous to the Union. I guess I'll just wait and see what happens next."

"Your secret is safe with me, Caroline," said Mollie. "We've always shared our secrets." Then she added, "I have some cold fried chicken, and corn bread and preserves you can take him when you go."

* * *

"Your friend, Mollie, is very kind," said Alex as he finished the last piece of corn bread. "Extend my thanks. Perhaps sometime I'll be able to meet her and thank her myself."

He had changed into the clothes Caroline had brought and removed the bandage from his head. The wound, healing well, was nearly hidden by his hair.

He is rather handsome, Caroline thought. He'd probably be very attractive after a shave.

"Will you be coming back tomorrow?" he asked.

"I'll manage somehow to get here and bring you something to eat. But now I have to go home to weed the garden."

"I'll be looking for you."

Next day, Caroline again took food to Alex. They talked of many things—more views on the war, their families, the spring now turning into summer, how they both liked wild strawberries, but he wouldn't drink buttermilk and she refused to eat mushrooms.

As she prepared to leave, Alex took her hand and pressed it to his lips.

"You are, indeed, an angel, little Caroline. I'll never forget what you've done."

She smiled. "I'll be back tomorrow. Rest well."

* * *

The next morning could not come fast enough for Caroline. She hurried through her tasks, humming softly as she worked. To her, it seemed the birds sang more cheerily than usual, the sun was brighter, the flowers more beautiful and more fragrant. As soon as she was able, she saddled Silky and was off. The horse seemed to fly down the road as though he had wings.

When she reached the shack, Caroline dismounted, calling, "Alex, I'm here!"

There was no reply.

"Alex?" she repeated as she stepped through the door. The bedding she had brought was folded. And Alex was gone.

Church bells pealed across the valley. Rain had fallen during the night but the clouds were breaking up, leaving patchy holes for sunbeams to stream through. Finches in the sycamore trees shook the leaves as they flitted to and fro in the branches, sending a shower of droplets on the Marchant buggy as it pulled up to the churchyard.

Caroline straightened her bonnet and alighted from the buggy. She picked up her skirts, carefully avoiding rain puddles as she walked to the door. Her father, with her mother on his arm, came up the steps behind her. They greeted friends who were assembling, and took their seat inside.

Oliver and Mollie entered with their children in tow. As they passed Caroline, Mollie handed her a small package.

"Here's your quilt pattern back, and thanks," she whispered. "There's something else for you, too."

Caroline started to open the paper, but Mollie quickly shook her head and hurried on down the aisle.

Home in her room, Caroline took the packet from her pocket and removed the string. Wrapped in the brown paper was the quilt pattern and an envelope addressed to Mollie, but the letter inside was to Caroline. She opened it quickly.

"My dear Caroline,

    I am sorry to have left so abruptly but it was necessary for me to do so. The longer I stayed, the greater was the risk of my being discovered. Again, my thanks for all the kindness you showed me. I promise I will find a way to repay you. It is not impossible that I shall see you again. I trust that is acceptable to you.

                           A. Cameron"

Chapter Five

The late August sun simmered over the Pennsylvania countryside. Spiders criss-crossed bushes with golden filaments. Weeds dried up along roads and trails, as birds began to congregate in the huge reunion that would precede their southern migration. Crickets under the leaves were tuning up for evening concerts which would grow in numbers of participants and in volume as evenings grew cooler. Frogs croaked their bass accompaniments between snapping at flies that circled over moss-filled streams.

All nature continued its annual processes, not concerned that man was busy in his bloody pursuit of what appeared to be an attempt to annihilate his kind in this year of 1863, with fighting between the forces of North and South at great intensity. Southern forces, invading Pennsylvania earlier in the year, had suffered a devastating defeat at Gettysburg. Vicksburg, Mississippi, had fallen to the Union, virtually cutting the Confederacy in half. Now the battle for Chattanooga, Tennessee, was beginning to take shape.

Tension was high in Pennsylvania. Although Gettysburg marked the only real attempt by the Confederates to invade that state, fear of another attempt was great. Cities, towns and even small villages were fortifying themselves. Yet living must continue. Farm crops must be harvested and the usual business of life must be attended to.

On this particular warm day, James Marchant and his wife, intent on keeping things normal in an abnormal situation, hitched up the buggy and rode into town. "Town" was Cross Corners, a village a number of miles from Uniontown located on Cross Creek, a small tributary to the navigable Monongahela River. The Marchant farm was situated to include the junction of a smaller stream to Cross Creek, the stream near which the shack that had sheltered the injured Rebel scout stood.

Caroline didn't go to Cross Corners with her parents, but stayed home to make preserves. All morning she had been busy at her task, and now she was hungry, for the work had taken part of the afternoon to complete. Wood from the woodbox was now gone and, to her dismay, she found none of the stove-length logs had been chopped for use.

33

Picking up a couple of small logs, Caroline started toward the chopping block. She was startled to hear her name called, and turned to see a tall man with a wide smile coming around the shed.

"May I help you with that?" he asked, and while Caroline stood staring in disbelief, he took the logs from her arms.

"Alex?" she stammered. "Is it really you?"

He gave a hearty laugh. "It is, in the flesh."

"I can hardly believe it," she said incredulously. "I never expected to see you again!"

"Nor I you, the truth be known," he replied. He took the axe from the block and, with a few powerful strokes, reduced the logs to burnable size for the stove. Alex was not now the pale, weak man she had nursed to health in the shack some time back, dirty, unshaven and bloody. His hair was bleached by the sun, his clean-shaven face tanned by days spent outdoors. And he was even taller than she remembered.

"Where would you like me to put this?" he asked as he loaded his arms with the wood.

"There's a woodbox in the kitchen," Caroline indicated the door, and they went in "There—by the stove."

Alex dropped the wood in the box and turned again to the young woman. He had watched her briefly from a distance until he was quite sure she was alone and he would be safe. He could not forget how kind she had been to him. He only vaguely remembered someone approaching him by the stream but he could not forget the cool water on his face, the gentle hands that raised his head to give him a drink. He still kept the handkerchief she had left wet on his forehead.

But he remembered in detail her daily visits, the food and medication she brought, and their conversations. She was small, only about five feet four inches, and he wondered how she was able to get him to that shack. He trusted her then, and he sincerely hoped that he could trust her now.

"I was just fixing myself something to eat. Would you care to join me?" she asked.

"Feeding me again. Yes, I'd be pleased."

As she fried pork and potatoes, and prepared carrots and fresh greens from the garden, he explained his sudden departure from the shack.

"I'm sorry I had to take my leave without telling you," he said, "but I just couldn't take a chance on being caught."

"Or being turned in?" Caroline asked, teasing.

"I don't think you would do that, even now." He put the dishes on the table.

"I like to think that I'm as patriotic as the next person, but you're right. I don't think I could ever turn you in." Then after a pause, "If I asked you about your mission, about whether you accomplished it, would you tell me?"

"For your sake as well as mine, I can't." Then he added, "Only this. I slipped out during the night and got to the Monongahela the next day. I found an obliging owner of a keel boat that let me go with him to Pittsburgh. My mission was, and still is, to gather information. I do a lot of moving around."

"All right." Caroline put the food on the table and watched as he ate. "What are you going to do now? Are you going back to Virginia? I'll never see you again."

"I'll see you again, angel. I *will* see you. But until this war is over, I don't know when."

"The war seems to be going badly for you. Union forces are making big advances. Perhaps it will be over soon."

"The war has reached a very crucial point, but it's far from over."

"Alex, let's not talk about the war. It's too upsetting."

He nodded his agreement before he asked, "How are your brothers?"

"Last we heard, they were well. The mails are not as regular as we'd like from soldiers on the move."

"This soldier on the move would like to hear from you."

"I'd love to hear from you, too, Alex. But how? There's no mail exchange allowed between Union and Confederate states."

"I can give you an address where your letters can get through to me without casting suspicion. Also, there's the 'flag of truce' exchanges between North and South, and a good amount of smuggling. And remember, I'm a scout and sometimes courier." She nodded her agreement. "But what about you?" he asked. "You've said your parents are extremely . . ." his voice trailed off. Before she could respond, he asked, "What about your friend, Mollie? Would it create problems if I wrote to you through her?"

"Like you did before? I think it would work. Mollie's my dearest friend, and I'm sure Oliver would agree." Caroline lowered her eyes. "I dislike not telling my parents, but there is no way I *can* tell them until the war is over."

The meal finished, Caroline and Alex walked hand in hand outside to the porch. For a brief while they continued to talk, since each seemed to want the moment to go on. Then they sat, just looking at each other, each studying a face that the fortunes of war had suddenly brought to them and could just as suddenly take away.

Finally Alex rose. "I must go," he said. He removed her handkerchief from his pocket. "But I have this to remember you by."

Caroline took the handkerchief and gently kissed it, her eyes never leaving his. She then pressed it to his lips. He pocketed the handkerchief, then took both her small hands in his and kissed them. Turning, he quickly left the porch and was gone. Caroline still stood long after he had disappeared from sight.

Mollie Cook sat listening quietly as Caroline poured out her story and watched her twisting her hands nervously. She loved this small blonde girl like a sister, and felt protective of her. They had been friends as teen-agers, and Mollie had watched Caroline grow into young womanhood. They had made quite a picture together—Caroline fair as sunlight and Mollie with her thick, dark locks and big brown eyes—giggling together and sharing secrets. Her marriage to Oliver Cook, who complemented her bubbly exuberance, did nothing to change their friendship.

"I hope it won't cause you problems if I should get letters from Alex," Caroline was saying. "I don't see how I would dare have anything mailed direct to me. Father would be sure to question me and then forbid me to have anything to do with Alex." She shuddered. "At the very least!"

"I'm your friend, aren't I?" asked Mollie, her words more a statement than a question. "Oliver needs to know, of course, but he cares as much about you as I do."

"Oh, Mollie. You are the dearest soul!" Caroline gave her friend a hug.

"I must meet that fine southern gentleman sometime. You love him, don't you?"

"Love him? I . . . I really don't know. I haven't really been able to sort out my thoughts about him. I helped Alex when he needed help, which made him special. And he was so kind and gracious." Caroline hesitated. "But still, he is an enemy of my country and he could be shot on sight as a Rebel scout. I don't know how much damage he may already have caused our side. And his Rebs did kill William."

"Love doesn't care which side of the war you're on," Mollie said. "And when you really love him, you won't have any question."

"One more thing bothers me, Mollie," Caroline continued. "Not telling my parents. I feel like a sneak, but how can I possibly tell them?"

Mollie gave her friend a comforting smile. "That's something you will have to work out. It's between your tender conscience, your good judgment and your parents. Providence has a strange way, sometimes, of solving our problems."

* * *

Caroline didn't hurry Silky on the way home. The horse walked slowly, kicking up small clouds of dust, its hooves clicking a staccato on the wooden bridge as it crossed. Below, a deer drinking from the creek looked up, water dripping from its muzzle, and watched the pair go by. Then it moved quickly down the creek bank past the swift water under the bridge to a shallower, less turbulent area to cross over and disappear into the trees.

"Smart deer," Caroline thought. "That's a dangerous crossing with such deep and swift currents by the bridge." But she didn't dwell on the thought. She was working out a plan.

That evening, Caroline and her mother sat in the parlor knitting socks. All the women in the village were knitting and doing whatever else they could do to help the war effort. There was hardly a family that didn't have someone serving in the army, as Pennsylvania had provided a much larger number of men than had been asked for. Her father soon joined his wife and daughter and settled himself in his favorite chair to read the latest paper out of Pittsburgh.

"Mother," Caroline broke the quiet of the room, "you know the story of the Good Samaritan in the Bible. Would you have helped the Samaritan if you had been there?"

Her mother looked up, "Who knows what we'll do in a given circumstance until we face it? But, of course, I'd like to think I would help. Why do you ask?"

"What if," Caroline continued carefully, "you should come upon someone lying beside the road to Cross Corners and he was hurt—bad? What would you do then?"

"I guess I'd try to help him. I must say, Caroline, I don't know what you're getting at." Maude Marchant's voice began to reveal curiosity. Her needles clicked faster.

"I found someone last spring lying by the creek just off the road, and I helped him. Was I wrong?"

"No, of course not. Who was it?"

At that point, James Marchant lowered his paper, his interest apparently aroused by the conversation.

"He was a stranger to me." Caroline kept her eyes on her work. "Should I have helped him and asked questions after, or should I have found out who he was first to determine if he was worth helping?"

"I must say, I don't know what you are talking about, daughter," her father interjected. "Is this an actual event or just something you made up for the sake of argument? Please explain yourself."

Caroline hoped that she had set the proper stage but she knew she would still have to proceed carefully. "As I said, last spring I found a man hurt and I helped him. He had been shot." She glanced up at her parents. "I came back to the house for help, and I overheard you talking about someone Barney had shot in town. That was the man I found."

"You found that spy?" Marchant asked incredulously, "and helped him?"

"Caroline, how could you?" her mother scolded. "I thought he was dead."

"Mother, I thought of Johnny and Charles. I knew if either of my brothers was hurt I'd want someone, even a Rebel, to help them. I just thought of them."

Caroline's expressed compassion appeared to be totally lost on her parents. Her mother appeared near tears and her father clenched his fists, crumpling the newspaper.

"Go on," he said tersely.

Her voice trembling, Caroline continued. "He was a human being in need and I couldn't just let him die there. I took him to the old trapper's shack and I went there to take care of him for a few days. But one night he just slipped away." The story was out now. Caroline felt a weight slip from her shoulders, but her palms were moist.

"You helped a spy?" her mother cried in horror. "You helped a devil that might have killed our William?"

"Oh, Mother, he didn't kill William. He's only a man caught up in this terrible war, the same as we are. It's just that he happened to be living in a secessionist state. He's just fighting for what he believes—the same as we are."

"But he's wrong, daughter!"

"Of course he's wrong in part of his philosophy. But we'll win the war, and then we'll have to heal all these wounds." Caroline put her knitting down. "He's not a demon. He's a human being!"

"You sound as though you know all about that Reb, like you got rather fond of him," her father persisted.

"We talked . . . shared ideas about why North and South are fighting."

"And you didn't tell us," he continued, anger again in his voice.

"I was afraid you'd react just the way you are now, and I didn't want to upset you." Caroline's voice was shaking. "I just couldn't go off and let the man die there!"

Her mother rocked back and forth in her chair, softly weeping. James Marchant leaned forward.

"Caroline," he said in a low, fierce voice, "if you ever have anything to do with any Reb again, you are no daughter of mine!"

Chapter Six

September 8, 1863

My dear Caroline,

Though it has been but two weeks since we last spoke, it seems forever. I remember your great kindness to me. You are the brightest sunshine in this gloomy business of war. I continue to travel. You understand why I cannot say more than I do. The war goes on and there is much suffering and death. Even though one would expect me to be hardened to these things now, I can hardly endure what I see. I pray for an end to this terrible tragedy. I hope for a peace that will not destroy the South. Yes, and I pray for the day I may see you again.

Regards to you,

Alexander C.

October 25, 1863

Dear Alex,

I know your letters must be few and also brief. I cherish each word you write. I, too, pray for an end to the war. My heart cries for the wounds of my beloved country, that we must be considered enemies when we are Americans all.

The country is beautiful this time of year. The hills are aflame with color, and ice now forms at the edges of the creek for a brief moment before the sun destroys it. Snow may not be far off.

My friend, Mollie, tells me she will have another child come spring. She is a dear mother to her two little boys. Her husband, Oliver, would join the army but for his bad knee, and now he is needed at home even more. Mollie is delighted about the baby. She hopes that she will have a daughter now.

Keep yourself safe for me.

With greatest concern,

Caroline

December 5, 1863

Dear Caroline,

Your words cheer me, and there is need for cheer these days. The Confederacy continues to suffer setbacks. You undoubtedly know of the defeat we suffered at Chattanooga and the Union losses at Chickamauga. In spite of our win there (and I know "our" means the Confederacy, and not your interests), things are going badly. Ever since Gettysburg last spring, we've had considerable setbacks. But we have not yet given up hope.

I was able to get home a few days ago. My father tried to put in his crops last spring but this war has laid the crops all to waste. When this war is over and we're able to put things back in order, I want to take you to my home. It's beautiful in the summertime. Have you ever been on a fox hunt? I would like to take you with me. I appreciate your frequent long letters.

Affectionately,

Alex

February 24, 1864

Dear Alex,

The winter is hard here, but it must be a sore trial to those in the armies, both yours and mine. I don't know how you are faring. You say all is well, and I truly hope it is. In spite of being cold and harsh, the snow is beautiful. The little tributary of Cross Creek that runs past the shack is frozen over, and the other day I watched a family of otters frolic on the ice. For a little while I forgot about the war.

I have not yet told my mother and father that you were here last fall nor that I am writing to you, only as I wrote you earlier that I helped you last spring. They would be so upset and angry. When will this war be over? I don't know how much longer I can bear it. Please be careful.

With my affection,

Caroline

With the advance of March, the withdrawal of winter was well under way. Its icy grip was being released, as seen in the softening of the snow, with muddy fields emerging. Icicles lengthened as snow water dribbled down, shortened as they fell away under the sun's rays and began to freeze again at evening. On the sunny side of houses and trees shoots from early bulbs poked their way to the air, and the first crocuses opened delicate petals.

And Alex again made his way to the Marchant farm. Caroline stood waiting for him, and watched as he rode up to the house. He dismounted, and she extended her hands, which he took in his. Then Alex tipped her face up in his hand and kissed her. Startled, Caroline pulled back. After all, in spite of their letters, this man was still a Reb and she'd only seen him on two occasions before. But she smiled.

"That's mighty bold of you, sir," teased Caroline as they walked to the house. "A Confederate scout coming right up to the house of a Yankee in broad daylight."

"We Confederate scouts are always bold and brave," he said with exaggerated bravado. Then more seriously, "I really felt that it was time that I met your parents and tried to clear things up."

"They're not here," answered Caroline, "and it's just as well. It just wouldn't work. Not yet."

"Did you deliberately get them to leave?"

"Yes, and it wasn't easy. But they'll be gone all day. I persuaded them this was the best day for them to go to Uniontown for Mother's quilt frames and for things Father needs for the farm."

"I hate to put you through all this for me."

"It's all right. And the time will come. But now we have a whole day for ourselves—a whole day for you to tell me everything that has happened to you."

"One day. Only one day." He shook his head. "It should be a lifetime instead." Alex reached into his pocket and pulled out a small white square of linen. "I still carry your handkerchief—and your kiss," he said as he held it up. "But I have something more. As I told you in my letters, I was able to get home on a short leave. I didn't tell you it was to attend my mother's funeral."

"Oh, Alex, no!"

"Mother was always frail, and she just became a victim of the war. So much of the fighting has been in surrounding areas, and it was too much for her. She took to her bed, gradually got weaker, and finally slipped away."

"I'm so sorry," Caroline said, thinking of how she would feel if she were to lose her own mother.

"She's at rest now," he replied.

Then Alex reached into another pocket and brought out a small folded cloth which he unfolded to take out a delicate gold ring. Apparently the ring had been worn a long time so that the gold had developed a beautiful patina. It was set with a small diamond on either side of a larger one.

"It's beautiful," Caroline said softly. "Your mother's?"

"Yes. And now I want you to have it."

Her fingers trembling, Caroline took the ring from the handkerchief. "They're real diamonds, aren't they?" she asked as she turned it in her fingers. "I've never held a diamond before."

"Look," Alex took the ring. He walked to the window and with the diamond carefully, in a high corner, cut A C, and under it C M, in the glass. " 'I love you' is too much to write, but every time you see this, you'll know."

Alex slipped the ring on her finger. "Caroline, I do love you. I want you to be my wife."

"Oh, yes, Alex, yes." Then she was in his strong arms and he was kissing her. "I love you, Alex, I love you."

Arm in arm, Alex and Caroline walked in the woods. They talked of many things—their families, his travels, early robins that scattered as they approached, a squirrel aroused from hibernation only to rush back into its hole in a tree as they approached, about Mollie and Oliver and the baby that was due any day. The war seemed far away. But it couldn't stay away.

Abruptly, Caroline asked, "What are we going to do when the war is over?"

"What do you mean, angel?"

"This bitterness between North and South won't end just because the shooting stops."

"You mean a Yankee girl won't be any more accepted in Virginia than a Confederate soldier would be in Pennsylvania? Yes, I've been thinking about that, too. I couldn't subject you to the hardships you'd have to bear in rebuilding the plantation, to say nothing of the people." He shook his head. "You can't believe what has happened there."

"I live on a farm. I know hard work."

"There isn't anyone who wouldn't love you when they got to know you."

"Spoken like a true Southern gentleman!" Caroline laughed.

Alex stopped to pick up a stone which was flat and smooth. Deftly, he threw it across the pond. The stone bounced five times on the water before sinking out of sight. Caroline picked up one, but her stone only sank with a plop.

She said, "Oh, dear. Johnny was a master of stone skipping, but I never could get the hang of it."

"Let me show you." With much laughter, a lesson in stone skipping followed, until Caroline finally got one to skip twice.

They sat on a log, and Alex took her small hands in his.

"Perhaps the best solution for us would be to start new somewhere else altogether," Alex mused aloud. "I wouldn't be accepted here any more than you would be there. Like you, I could endure it, and perhaps win out in the end, but . . ." His voice trailed off.

"But what about your plantation? And," she added in mock seriousness, "you did promise me a fox hunt."

"My brother—he's older, you know—would take care of that. He'd be able to help Father and be most happy to. He's always loved the plantation as much as I have. And some of our slaves have stayed."

"Do you really want to give up your home?"

"You'd be giving up yours, too, and your family."

"I guess when we have each other, that's all we really need, isn't it?"

He nodded his agreement. "As long as we have each other."

* * *

Caroline, fearing the repercussions if she told her parents about Alex's visit, removed the ring and put it on a ribbon around her neck. Her heart was light. To be loved by someone whom she loved with all her heart was joy unspeakable. She knew now what Mollie had meant when she said that if she really loved Alex, there would be no question about her love.

She would have to see Mollie tomorrow, to share her happiness. Mollie would really be surprised. She hadn't even known Alex was coming. His letter was so uncertain that Caroline, herself, almost dared not hope he'd be able to come, and she had said nothing to Mollie.

But the clouds of war still hung over them. Caroline often thought of how she would love to share her happiness with her mother, to make together plans and preparations for her wedding. Her mother's deft fingers could fashion a most beautiful wedding gown, and they would have the closeness that only a future bride and her mother could know.

Caroline knew this couldn't be. Years of war had taken their toll, in the deaths of William and many other brave men on both sides, in fear and in hate born of fear. The end of the war would not make much difference, either, at least not for a long time. How ironic, she thought, that the very thing that had brought her and Alex together was marring their happiness and tearing their families apart. Was she wrong to love Alex so when the family she loved so much would be hurt by her love for Alex?

Caroline was still mulling the situation over in her mind when she heard her parents' buggy drive into the yard. She remembered that she had promised to have supper ready when they returned. She hurried downstairs to try to get something started before they came in. There would be a few minutes while her father put the horses in the barn.

But before she could get potatoes out of the bin, the door flew open. James Marchant came in half carrying his wife. Maude was pale, her eyes closed, and she leaned heavily on her husband. His own face was pale and grim.

Gently he placed her in an armchair and barked to Caroline, "Get water for your mother!"

"Yes, Father." Caroline hurried for a cup. "What's wrong with her? What's happened?"

"She's had a shock. We both have," he said as he removed his wife's bonnet and shawl, and loosened her collar. "Go tend to the horses. We've driven hard from Cross Corners."

"But Mother . . ."

"Do as I say! Now!"

Caroline hurried to do her father's bidding, tears stinging her eyes. What had happened? Why wouldn't he tell her? She unhitched the buggy, put the team in the barn, hastily threw a couple of forkfuls of hay in the manger for them, and ran back to the house.

Maude was in bed, a damp cloth on her forehead.

"I think she'll rest now," said James. He left the bedroom and closed the door.

"Father, tell me! What's happened?"

James turned to Caroline. His eyes were wet but anger and hate showed through the tears.

"You and your Rebel spy!" he shouted. "You! Helping the enemy!"

"Father, oh Father!" Caroline cried.

"Coming through Cross Corners, we stopped at the town hall to see why such a crowd was gathered there. They were looking at a new casualty list in the Pittsburgh paper that had just arrived."

Caroline caught her breath.

In anguish, he continued, "Johnny's been killed!"

Caroline threw her arms around her father, and together they wept.

Chapter Seven

For nearly two weeks, Maude Marchant kept to her bed although no official notification was received concerning the death of John Marchant. The list in the newspaper was the only word they had. James was grim but the farm demanded his attention.

Caroline said little. At times she went to the window, pretending to look out but instead she stared at the initials scratched high in the corner. At night, in her room, she would take out the ring and put it on her finger. She watched the stone sparkle in the lamplight, and she would hold the ring to her cheek. And almost always there were tears.

She didn't tell Mollie of the visit from Alex until after the birth of Mollie's tiny black-haired, brown-eyed Betsy. Caroline had gone to visit Mollie, and she sat rocking the infant while Mollie mended trousers for her boys.

"Mollie," she asked, "could Alex really be considered responsible for—what happened to Johnny and William?"

"Oh, I don't know," Mollie said thoughtfully. "I think it's just the fortunes—or misfortunes—of war. I mean, how can we tell how any information Alex gathered affected the war?"

"The war is going badly—for them, I mean—so maybe it wasn't all that much," Caroline continued. She hesitated. "I guess what I'm trying to say is that Alex was back a few weeks ago."

"And you didn't tell me?"

"He—he asked me to marry him."

Mollie looked up in surprise, her needle still. "He did? What did you tell him?"

"I told him yes, but—oh, Mollie, now I don't know. That same night we learned about Johnny."

"What's troubling you, little friend? There's something more."

"Father called me a traitor for helping Alex that time, and I've been wondering now—was I really? I didn't take his accusation seriously until Johnny . . . but now . . . I don't know. And how can I marry someone who may have been even partly responsible for the deaths of my two brothers?"

Gently Mollie put the sleeping baby in her cradle. Then she knelt in front of Caroline and took her hands.

"How many southerners do you think are mourning the loss of sons, brothers and husbands that may have been the victims of Charles, and William and Johnny? I know that Oliver was excused from the draft because of that bad knee, and because of me and our babies. But you and I both know that if it weren't for that, my husband would be out there with the rest of the men. And he wouldn't hesitate to shoot."

Caroline nodded in silent agreement as Mollie continued.

"Would you think less of Charles if he should marry a pretty little southern belle and bring her back?"

Caroline said slowly, "I really thought I was in love with Alex, but what happened to Johnny has really affected me . . ."

"When the time comes, you'll know." Mollie gave her a hug. "Now tell me all about what happened."

And Caroline could only hope that Mollie was right.

* * *

An early June day dawned on an almost perfect scene. The sky was a blue that went on forever. Fields planted in the spring were thriving, with their patchworks of green tinting the landscape. Hillsides were bursting with new growth, while wild flowers bloomed in bright patches of color everywhere. It was a day that seemed to have been created to show what heaven might be like.

Caroline spent the morning weeding the garden. Now, in the warm early afternoon, she left peas and beans to cool herself at the creek. Water chattering as it rippled over the rocks was enticing, so enticing, in fact, that she took off her shoes and carefully tested the water with one toe. It was so refreshing that she lifted her skirts and stepped into the water. Oh, how wonderful the swift coolness felt!

She looked around to take in the beauty that surrounded her, and then caught a glimpse of her reflection in the stream. She moved, and the picture shattered into a thousand diamonds. She stood very still, and the surface became smooth except for little rills around her bare legs. How daring of her to expose her legs up to mid-calf! She laughed aloud.

She could see in her reflection that her hair had lost some of its pins and was beginning to fall around her ears. Not yet willing to leave the cool water, she poked the top edge of her skirt up under her sash to keep the hem out of the water, freeing her hands to fix the stray locks. Then she changed her mind and let her hair fall soft and full around her shoulders and down her back. She reached for the sky, stretching upward as though to hold the day and never let go.

On a small rise not far away, a man on horseback watched. She was the most beautiful creature he thought he'd ever seen, her hair golden in the sun, her bare arms outstretched, the hem of her dress blue as the sky, dipping ever so lightly into the stream. He urged his horse with a dig of his heels, and they moved almost noiselessly down toward her.

Caroline suddenly felt someone near, watching her. Quickly, she lowered her arms and looked around. Riding toward her on a big bay horse was Alex Cameron.

Caroline drew in her breath in surprise. Hesitating only a moment, she stepped out of the water and ran toward him. In one leap, Alex was off the horse, running toward her. He caught Caroline in his strong arms, and lifted her off the ground. They embraced, Caroline standing tiptoe on his dusty boots in her bare, wet feet, the water from her skirts making rivulets on the ground.

They clung to each other, willing the moment never to end. He buried his face in her hair, then tilting her face up to him with a finger under her chin, he kissed her again and again.

"Caroline, marry me—now, today," Alex whispered.

"Yes, yes, yes!"

With a whoop and a holler, he swung up on his horse and pulled her up behind him.

"My shoes!" she exclaimed.

"Never mind about them. I'll buy you new ones!"

"What with? Confederate money?"

And they were off, Alex laughing, Caroline shrieking, clinging to him, her arms around him much tighter than they needed to be, both of them knowing that and loving it.

They rode swiftly, as if the big bay had sprouted wings, the young couple on his back shouting and laughing like children estatic with happiness. Finally they slowed to a more reasonable pace.

"Where are we going?" Caroline asked breathlessly.

"Where's the nearest preacher, my barefoot bride?"

"There's Reverend Keiler in Cross Corners."

"We'll go there!"

"Oh, no!" she exclaimed. "I can't risk having my husband get shot on our wedding day!"

"Only a few people have ever seen me and they wouldn't remember me after this long. Don't worry, my angel."

"Just the same, I'd rather go to Mollie and Oliver's place. They'll help us."

Alex patted the hands that were tight around his waist. "Okay, dear heart. Tell me where to go."

She rubbed her cheek on his strong back. "Anyway, I don't have any shoes. I can't get married without shoes."

Oliver was sharpening his tools on the grindstone in the yard as Alex and Caroline rode in. They hailed him with such exuberance that Mollie came running out to see what the excitement was about. With hugs, handshakes and squeals, introductions were made, the news shared and congratulations offered.

"We can have the wedding here." Mollie's eyes sparkled with excitement.

"I'll hitch up the buggy and go bring Reverend Keiler here—kidnap him if I have to." Oliver turned to the barn, but Alex called him back.

Handing him the necessary money, Alex said, "Buy shoes for my bride. She won't get married without them." Then, because of Caroline's earlier remark, he added, "It's strictly Union money," and squeezed her.

"Oh, Oliver," Caroline's face lost it's smile for a moment, "will you tell my parents? They won't come. I'm sure they won't. But I want them to know I love them and want them here. I'm sure they'll take it better from you than from me."

"Sure." Oliver patted her arm and went for the buggy.

"All right, Caroline," said Mollie, "let's see if we can make my wedding dress fit you before Oliver gets back." Then turning to Alex with a twinkle in her eye, she commented, "Alex, bridegrooms are just in the way at times like this. You can be my baby sitter."

* * *

Oliver went first to the Marchant farm. Get the hardest thing over with first, he thought. Both James and Maude Marchant were at the house when he arrived, and they welcomed Oliver cordially.

"Caroline is at our place," he said. "She has asked me to bring you some news." Oliver told the Marchants of Alex's visits to Caroline and the pending marriage. "She knew how upset you'd be if you knew, so she didn't tell you before. She asked me to bring you to the wedding. Will you come?"

James Marchant and his wife were silent, their faces showing their stunned astonishment by Oliver's account. Mrs. Marchant rocked back and forth in her chair, dabbing frequently at tears that fell. As Oliver finished his story, Mr. Marchant swore under his breath, then he picked up the item nearest his hand—a china pitcher—and threw it violently at the door.

"Well, I can't turn him in," Marchant said, his teeth clinched. "Not now."

"Please come," Oliver urged. "Caroline would be so happy."

"She will never hurt my wife again." James helped Maude to her feet. "From this moment, we have no daughter." His arm around his wife's shoulders, he led her from the room.

Caroline and Alex were married late in the afternoon at the home of Oliver and Mollie Cook. Oliver literally kept his word about kidnapping the preacher, getting him in the buggy by telling him there was an urgent need for him. He explained the situation to the cleric as they rode back to the farm. A confirmed romantic himself, Reverend Keiler agreed to perform the ceremony.

Caroline was dressed in the white satin gown Mollie had worn at her wedding. True, the gown was four inches too long, and was pinned in at the waist and hastily tucked in here and there to fit Caroline's more petite frame. A wreath of white daisies and red roses from the garden sat daintily on the little bride's long blonde hair. Caroline carried a bouquet of daisies, columbines and spicy-smelling pinks, and Mollie had put vases filled with spring flowers around the room.

Alex, scrubbed and polished, was dressed in Oliver's good suit which gave the appearance of both a southern gentleman and a Pennsylvania farmer. He looked at Caroline and his heart swelled within him. This lovely little thing had given so much to him and was willing to give up so much more. Did he really have the right to ask it of her? Yet he knew, they both knew, they would have it no other way. The war had brought them together and they would not permit it to separate them. They belonged together.

Reverend Keiler began, "Dearly beloved, we are gathered together . . ."

Mollie and Oliver held hands and exchanged glances with smiles to show they were remembering their own wedding. Their two little sons, Ollie and Henry, sat wide-eyed on the couch. Ollie poked Henry, got poked back, but a poke by their father settled them down. Baby Betsy slept right through the ceremony.

"Repeat after me," the minister continued, "I, Alexander, take thee, Caroline . . ."

"I, Alexander, take thee, Caroline . . ."

Again, "I, Caroline, take thee, Alexander . . ."

"I, Caroline, take thee, Alexander . . ."

"Do you have the ring? the minister asked.

Caroline took the ring he had given her from the ribbon around her neck.

"With this ring, I thee wed . . ." Reverend Keiler continued.

"With this ring, I thee wed . . ."

"I now pronounce you man and wife . . . 'til death do you part."

Alex swept Caroline into his arms, brushing aside the risk of being stuck by pins, and gave her a tender kiss. She was again off her feet, and Mollie's slightly too large satin wedding slippers slid to the floor. The bride was, again, shoeless.

Reverend Keiler stayed for the wedding supper that Mollie had prepared—cold sliced ham, fried chicken, bread and butter, and strawberries just picked, with sugar and fresh cream.

While they were eating, Oliver asked, "What are your plans now, Alex? Do you have a place to go tonight, and how long before you have to return to your post?"

"Are there lodgings in Cross Corners we could get?" Alex asked, "or perhaps it would be better to go on to Uniontown?"

"Oliver," interjected Mollie, "couldn't they stay at McPartlands? At least for tonight rather than go all that way to Uniontown at this hour."

"See why I married her?" Oliver grinned. "She's not only beautiful, she's an organizer." To Mollie, "That's a great idea."

"Who, and where, are the McPartlands?" Alex asked.

"They have the next farm over. I'm taking care of their livestock until they get home tomorrow night. They went to Pittsburg for a couple of days."

"Is that all right with you, Mrs. Cameron?" Alex took her hand. "Then we can go on to Uniontown for a few days before I have to leave."

"Anything you say, Mr. Cameron." Caroline gave a little shiver of delight at the sound of the name he'd called her. She felt that the only thing that could possibly make her happier at this moment would be the presence of her parents. She chose not to think about the depth of the breach that might now separate her from them. Oliver had said nothing about his visit to the Marchants and, for the present, she chose not to ask.

Chapter Eight

June 18, 1864

Dear Alexander, my husband,

How strange it is to write that, and how wonderful! It seems impossible that two weeks ago I was home with my parents, not knowing if I would ever see you again. Now I know that you will always come to me. When the war is over, we will never again be separated. Oh, how I pray for an end to the war!

I have memories to sustain me until you come again. Weren't Mollie and Oliver grand to do all they did for us? How glad I am that you were finally able to meet them, and they, you. They gave us such a beautiful wedding on absolutely no notice at all. It was so good of them to let us stay at the McPartlands. I promise never to burn your breakfast eggs again, but you must promise not to tease and distract me.

I keep thinking of walking by your side down the streets of Uniontown during the few days we were there. No one knew us and we had no need to be afraid. Oh, this is what it will be like, I know, when we are once again together and this dreadful war is over.

I must tell you, I have moved to Mollie's. Oliver didn't tell me what happened at home until after we got back to Mollie's from Uniontown and you were on your way. When he asked my mother and father to attend our wedding, Father disowned me and Mother did not object. It breaks my heart but, even knowing this, I would have married you. I love you so.

Under the circumstances, I couldn't remain there longer. Oliver took me home in the wagon to get my things, and I have moved into the little bedroom over the kitchen. We found my shoes where I had left them on the creek bank, not much the worse for lying there for a week. The ones you bought me I am keeping for Sunday best.

Although my heart aches for needing the love of my parents, it is most pleasant being with Mollie, working alongside her and helping her with the children. We must some day find a way to repay their goodness.

Your loving Caroline

July 10, 1864

Dearest Caroline,

Your words have cheered me, although I regret deeply causing a rift between you and your parents. I promise you, my darling angel, I will do all in my power to reunite you when I am able to come again. I don't know how we can possibly repay all that the Cooks have done for us, but certainly we will do everything in our power. We owe them so much. We began our marriage in borrowed clothes and a borrowed home, but it will not always be so.

The war continues its bloody course. The Union general, Grant, continues to fire on Richmond. There's a very heavy loss of life. The Confederate forces hang on valiantly, but I despair for them. I can't see that the Confederacy will win, and I wish that they would call a halt and spare the lives of the valiant men on both sides, and come to some sort of an agreement.

But no more of this sadness. I, too, remember with pleasure the few days we had together. I won't care how many eggs you burn as long as I am with you. Oh, how I love you, my dearest one. I have asked so much of you, and you have given up so much and asked so little. I pray my love will sustain you until we are together again.

With deepest affection,

Alex

P.S. My father isn't as unhappy with having a Yankee daughter-in-law as I had thought he might be. You'll win him over easily.

October 9, 1864

My beloved husband,

Each season in Pennsylvania is the most glorious, and autumn this year is the most glorious of all. Never have the leaves been such a brilliant red, gold and purple. There are bushels of apples from the orchards and piles of orange squashes and pumpkins in the fields. Mollie makes a delicious pumpkin pie! The days are nearly as warm as summer, but the nights are crisp. Ice laces the edge of the creek in the early mornings, and the wild animals are getting nice thick coats for the winter.

But my rapture is in more than the beauty of God's nature. It is even more in the beauty of his miracles. You see, my dearest, we are to have a child. I have not told you before because I didn't want to worry you, but my joy is so great that I must share it. I can maintain my silence no longer.

I'm sure my mother knows of my condition, but she continues to deny that I exist. In a town as small as this, the news of our marriage was soon known, although it is known only that my husband is a stranger to the area. Neither Oliver and Mollie nor I have disclosed your identity beyond your name. My parents could never bring themselves to admit to anyone your allegiance. So people know only that they are unhappy with me.

Oh, how happy I am, even though my clothes begin to be uncomfortable. I rock tiny Betsy in my arms and pretend that she is our child already here, and dream of when I will actually hold our baby.

I read in the papers about the war and I worry about you. I am so grateful that you are a scout rather than in the actual fighting. Scouting's dangerous, too, I know, but at least you are not on the firing line. We have discussed this several times, so you know my strong allegiance to the Union.

Keep yourself safe from harm until you can come to us.

Lovingly, your

Caroline

November 28, 1864

Beloved Caroline,

Why didn't you tell me the wonderful news before? Never mind. You have already explained. But I am so excited! My darling, we are starting a new generation. I have been thinking for quite some time about the possibility of you and I starting out somewhere new when the war is over. We even discussed it briefly one time, you'll remember. With a child coming now, I feel even more strongly about it. What would you think about moving west somewhere? I understand there's land aplenty along the Ohio, or we could go down the Mississippi, perhaps to St. Louis or New Orleans. There are all sorts of possibilities. Where would you like to go, and what would you like to do? Think about it and let me know.

Have you thought about a name for our child? If we have a son, I would like to name him for your brother, William, to honor him for the sacrifice of his life. If it is a girl, she must be named for you, my angel.

As you may know, the Yankee general, Sherman, has been battering his way through Georgia. I have seen some of what he has done, and it is tragic. Even you, my Yankee sweetheart, would cry. Lincoln talks of rebuilding the South, but, if this continues, it will have to be rebuilt from the very soil. Sherman will achieve his goal of cutting the South in half, but at such a bloody cost!

But never mind. Take good care of yourself and our child. I love you and long to see you.

Your Alex

January 7, 1865

Alex, my dearest,

Your letters get fewer, which I know is because of the terrible situation with the Confederacy, now that there is so little hope for them. Perhaps your letters just don't get to me. I continue to write weekly, and more as I can, and hope that they reach you.

Two days ago we waited out a blizzard that swept the countryside, and today I took our child for a walk in the beauty it left. As though, not yet born, our baby could learn to love nature as we do! But it was beautiful. The creek was frozen over, and the otters that live there were sliding on it. I wanted to join them, but it was hard enough just to walk in the deep snow when I am so awkward now. I had to content myself with absorbing the glory of everything coated with ermine, the sun creating brilliant diamonds, sleigh bells somewhere off in the distance. Even my breath condensing in the cold delighted me.

The baby will be no stranger to me when he comes. I have learned so much just feeling him move and grow within me. It was so generous of you to want to name him William for my brother, and so his name shall be William Alexander Cameron. Or, should we have a daughter, Mary Caroline, for your mother.

Oliver went to Uniontown the other day and came back with some information about the farming country available in Ohio. He and Mollie are seriously considering moving there this spring. He feels that there would be opportunity available there that he is unable to realize here. I'm fairly certain that they will go, and, if they should, what would you like me to do? They have said that I am welcome to go with them until such time as you are free to come for me. Or I can make arrangements to stay here. Should I go to Virginia to your family? Where we go after we are together makes little difference to me as long as we are together.

Thank you for the money. I know it is hard for you to come by any to send now. Oliver says I more than earn my keep in helping Mollie, and the farm produces enough for all.

Keep yourself safe, my dearest. I miss you so.

Lovingly,

Caroline

February 18, 1865

My angel,

It is only a matter of time until the war is over. The Confederacy is about to crumble, but the wounds will be a long time healing, I'm afraid. I have seen so much misery and horror that sometimes I can't even sleep. My letters are less frequent because of lack of paper, the little pleasant news I have, and all the rest. It's all terribly depressing, and I hate to pass it on to you. Your cheerful letters—and at times they come in handfuls—are all that keep me going sometimes.

I feel, dearest, that it would be best for you to go with Mollie and Oliver when they go to Marietta. It separates us even more but you'll be safer there with our baby until I can come, which I hope will be soon. I want no more of this blood-soaked country. The memories are too painful. Unless you feel strongly otherwise, I feel we should go to Oregon, or perhaps California. We need a whole new life for ourselves and our baby.

I become more anxious for you as the birth draws near. Tell our friends that I'll spend my life trying to repay them for all they have done for us. Take good care of yourself for me.

Love and affection,

Alex

March 12, 1865

My beloved Alex,

We have a son. Our darling William Alexander was born night before last, and he took his sweet time about it. But he is worth all the waiting. Already I have forgotten the pain. He is beautiful, he is perfect, he is unique! Oh, yes, all mothers say that, but our William is different. He really is! Our son has a full head of soft golden fuzzy hair, the color of yours. And his eyes are blue. He has your smile but my nose. Or at least, I think it will be. Right now it is the cutest little button nose you ever saw! I could write volumes about him. I pray you can come soon to see him—and me!

I was in town a week or so before the baby was born, and saw my mother. For the first time, she didn't just look right through me. Our eyes met, and she seemed to want to speak. I told her I'd let her know when the baby came, and she just turned and walked away. It is painful for us both, and it's good, I guess, that we have seen so little of each other.

Mollie and Oliver are beginning to get ready for the move. He has obtained a flatboat and will take it down the Monongahela to Pittsburgh and thence down the Ohio to Marietta. The farmland he wants is just north of there a little ways. Anything he can't get on the boat he'll sell so as to have cash for their needs there.

Mollie's children are surely growing. Little Betsy is walking now and trying to say a few words. They consider William to be their own, even though his appearance is a contrast to their dark hair and eyes.

Take care of yourself, and please come to me soon. I miss you.

Your loving

Caroline and William

March 20, 1865

My angel Caroline and dear son,

Thank God for you both! I long to hold you and our infant son in my arms and tell you how much I love you. Thank you, Caroline, for giving me a strong, handsome son. Of course, he is unique! Look who his mother is. She is beautiful. No wonder he is as cute as a button.

When the war is over, and that should be soon now, I'll come to Marietta for you, and we three will head west to California. We'll begin again, and this time we'll have a proper life. We'll give our William a new heritage away from all this blood and sorrow.

I have been transferred from courier to the fighting forces. They have been so depleted—deaths, desertions, prisoners of war, and all—that they need every possible person manning a gun. But don't worry about me. From my position as a courier, I know the end is soon.

Deepest love and affection,

Alexander

Chapter Nine

As the days grew closer for the move to Ohio, Caroline became more anxious and impatient. Of course, foremost in her mind was to be reunited with Alex, with the war no longer to separate them. Lee had surrendered to Grant on April 9, and this was followed on April 18 by the armistice signed between Johnston and Sherman.

Caroline had not heard from Alex in several weeks, but she wasn't terribly concerned as yet, since long silences had happened before, and then suddenly several letters would arrive at the same time. And now, with the hostilities over but for a few pockets of resistance, she felt the danger for Alex was past.

Not that the hostile attitudes of the people on either side had suddenly subsided with the ending of the conflict. Angry feelings would be a long time ending.

In Cross Corners they were still high, and there had been no attempt by the Marchants to mend the rift between themselves and their daughter. Caroline met her mother one day in town and offered to bring William to the Marchant farm since she had left him with Mollie that day. Maude Marchant just sadly shook her head and turned away.

Caroline had even considered just hitching up the buggy and going to her parents anyway, hoping the sight of their infant grandson would soften her parents' hearts. But she decided not to go. Such a visit might only aggravate the unhappy situation. Her father could be very stubborn, and Caroline knew her mother wouldn't oppose him.

Perhaps when Charles came home he could help reunite Caroline with her parents. She had, of course, written to her brother to tell him of her marriage when she moved in with the Cooks, knowing that their parents were not likely to mention her in their letters to him. He had written back to say that he was sympathetic with her situation, but felt that it would be better for him not to try to intercede for her until he got home. Caroline knew that Charles loved her and that he would forgive her for marrying a man who was presently considered an enemy. Caroline knew Charles loved his country—the whole country—and that he fought to preserve it and that he would work just as hard to help heal the war's terrible wounds.

The townsfolk, of course, knew that there was a breach between Caroline and her parents, that Caroline was married to a stranger and, eventually, that there was a baby expected. Caroline stayed away from town as much as possible, and when she went to church she and the Cooks avoided discussing her marriage and her estrangement from her parents. Caroline was sure that some wondered if her husband was a Confederate but there was no way they could confirm such suspicions.

Caroline felt that the sooner she could get away from Cross Corners, the better the situation would be. She knew her presence had not been easy for Mollie and Oliver even though they never said so, and the anticipation of their move to Ohio helped to sustain them all.

Oliver was busy getting the farm ready for its new owners, while Caroline helped Mollie in the chore of deciding which of their possessions to keep and what they would have to give away or sell. Caroline continued to receive money from time to time from Alex, some of which she used to support herself and William, and some she put away for the trip.

"Let's keep the clothes the boys have outgrown," Mollie said one day near departure time. "William can have them as he grows into them." She picked up a little shirt with both elbows out. "Well," she demured, "maybe a few of them will do better as housecleaning rags."

"Oh, Mollie," Caroline suddenly burst out, "you are so good. You've done so much for me! I don't know how I can ever repay you." She sank down on a wooden box they were to pack, her face in her hands.

Mollie put her arms around her friend. "Caroline," she said, "you'd have done the same for me. Neither of us ever had a sister. Perhaps Providence in his goodness brought us together here in Cross Corners so we could be sisters to each other. You are just my little sister, and I love you dearly."

Caroline kissed Mollie's cheek. "Yes, I'm sure that's true. It seems fated to be so." She picked up Henry's baptism dress and folded it carefully.

"Mollie," she continued, "if anything ever happens to me, I want you to take William. If something happens on the way to Ohio, keep him for Alex. Promise me!"

Mollie laughed. "You worry too much. Nothing's going to happen."

"Promise!"

"I promise." Mollie picked up a small pair of shoes. "But you'll forget all about such a silly worry when you are together with Alex and the baby in California."

"Maybe we can persuade Oliver to move all of you out there with us."

With a laugh and a hug, the two young women busied themselves again with the packing.

May moved into the Pennsylvania countryside, bringing with it mild temperatures, longer days, and bright flowers everywhere. The wild creatures in the hills were bringing out their young for a first look at the outside world. Birds were busy filling the cavernous mouths of their chicks, and squirrels scurried here and there, seeking tidbits and scolding intruders.

Oliver had set the date of departure for one of the first days of the month, and all things seemed to be ready. The farm's new owners wanted to get in their crops, and Oliver wanted to do the same in the Ohio Valley. The day before the scheduled departure, he stopped at the post office on a final errand, to leave a forwarding address for himself and also one for Caroline.

"Everything will be taken care of," the postmaster assured him. "Oh, here's today's mail for you." He handed Oliver three letters.

Oliver glanced at them quickly. There was a letter from the land company, one from his brother already in Ohio, and the third to Caroline from Charles. She would be disappointed that again there were none from Alex. He glanced out the door at the sky.

"Storm's coming," he commented. "Hope it doesn't delay our starting. We're going to try to get away tomorrow."

The postmaster observed, "Storms this time of year can be hard, as you know, but they usually pass fast. You should be fine."

* * *

Caroline was disappointed at not receiving any letters from Alex. But the one from Charles made up for it. She opened it and read:

Dear sister Caroline,

I have unbelievable news! Our brother Johnny is not dead, as we had been led to believe. He has been a prisoner of war for the past year, and somehow has not been able or was not permitted to get word to us. I found him in a hospital. He's in poor shape and unable to tell me anything, but the doctors say he will recover in time. I don't know when he or I will be home.

I am letting you know about this so that you can tell our mother and father. I believe this will help you to improve your relationship with them. Please let them know immediately. The government will give them official notification and I will write, too, of course. But I want to give you this opportunity.

I am well and anxious to be home and help Father. I wish you and baby William well on your trip. I am sorry that I will not see you before you go.

With affection,

Your brother, Charles

Caroline wept tears of joy. Her thoughts were all a jumble. If only she could let Alex know! Why had she not heard from him for so long? How good Charles was to give her this opportunity!

"I must go now to tell Mother," she exclaimed, and ran to the barn to get a horse. Mollie and Oliver followed.

"Be careful," Oliver warned, glancing skyward again. "That storm doesn't look good. If it breaks, stay there overnight."

"Yes," added Mollie, "I'll take care of William."

"Oh, I'll be back. We want to get an early start tomorrow. I must be there to meet Alex." She prodded the horse and it went down the road at a gallop.

She had not gone far when the first raindrops started. She was glad to have the slicker Oliver had tossed to her at the last minute. As she reached Cross Creek bridge, she noticed that the water was very high and running swiftly. This is not just spring runoff, she thought. The storm must have been fierce in the hills. Well, rage on, water. Nothing will stop me now.

She crossed the bridge safely, then rode on. By the time she reached the Marchant farm, the storm had struck in its fury. The wind shrieked and the rain came down in sheets, but Caroline ignored it. She ran to the house and threw open the door.

"Mother, Mother!" she called, "Johnny's not dead! He's alive! Johnny's alive!"

Mrs. Marchant, at the cupboard, turned quickly, dropping the plate she was holding. It fell to the floor and shattered.

"No! Johnny's dead. What are you talking about?"

James Marchant appeared in the doorway. "What's going on here?"

Caroline repeated, "Johnny's alive! This letter came from Charles. He's found Johnny!" She held out the letter.

Mr. Marchant grabbed the letter and unfolded it. Maude hurried to him, and Caroline watched their faces as they read the good news. They clung together and, as she had done, they wept.

"Oh, my Johnny, my Johnny," Mrs. Marchant repeated over and over. Her husband held her in his arms.

Caroline waited a moment until they were calmer before she spoke. "Charles said, as you read, that he wanted me to break the news in the hopes that you would accept me again." The Marchants looked up as she continued. "Tomorrow morning, early, we—Oliver, Mollie and I—will be on our way to the Ohio Valley. I'm sure you know about the trip. I could go much happier if I knew you could forgive me for disappointing you so."

She stood there, water from the slicker dripping on the floor, her tears mixing with rain on her face. The elder Marchants didn't hesitate, but together they went to her, embraced, and cried with her.

The postmaster was right. The storm, though fierce, seemed to be moving over fast. Caroline sat at the kitchen table while she told her parents about Alex, about the baby, about Alex's insistence that he be named for William, and of their plans to meet in Ohio and go on to California and a new life. For a brief while Caroline and her parents were at peace.

Caroline glanced out the window. "The storm seems to be clearing. I'd better hurry back before dark."

"Can't you stay overnight until the weather is better?" her mother asked. "There's so much to catch up on."

I can't," Caroline said. "My baby will be hungry and I wouldn't want to hold up Oliver tomorrow morning anyway." She rose and picked up the slicker.

"I wish you'd reconsider," her father joined in.

"Thanks, but I don't think I'd better. Oh, there's one thing before I go . . ." She walked to the window and drew back the curtain. There in the glass were the initials Alex had cut with the diamond so many months ago. Her mother, seeing them, smiled.

As Caroline started back, the sun, low in the sky, broke through the clouds for a moment. But the storm hadn't completely moved on. There was still a mist in the air. Water dripped from the branches of the trees, splashed in the puddles on the road, and ran in rain-punctuated streams down the gutters. If she hurried, she thought, she could be back to her baby before dark.

Caroline urged the horse on. The bridge was near. She could hear angry water racing beneath it, but she wasn't worried. She had ridden this road so many times that every bend, every rise was like an old friend.

Caroline's mind was filled with the joyful reunion with her parents. There was so much more she had wanted to share with them. Perhaps they would come and see her off in the morning. She gave a little shiver of joy at the thought of showing their grandson to them.

The bridge appeared ahead of her, and she started to cross. At that moment, a final lightning bolt struck simultaneously with a loud crash of thunder. With a terrified scream, the horse reared up, bolted for the far side of the bridge and into the hills. As it reared, Caroline was pitched off. She fell headlong into the raging stream.

Chapter Ten

Kaye anticipated the ending of the General Assembly. Wade had given her a beautiful diamond engagement ring, one he had ordered designed especially for her, but they had not yet set a date for their wedding. Wade was deeply involved in hotly contested budget and banking issues before the assembly, and he wanted to wait until the session was over and they could see how the result would affect his future in running for Congress before setting a date.

This indecision was a disappointment to Kaye. Of course, she realized that all these activities would monopolize Wade's time, and she firmly believed in what he was fighting for. Her work load at the office would also be increased because of his extended absences. Still, her planning efforts toward her wedding would necessarily be quite limited without a date set.

So it was with anticipation that Kaye had dinner with Wade shortly after the session ended. They went to his club on a Sunday afternoon. As they ate, Wade described the activities of the assembly. The banking bill he considered dangerous had been defeated, and he felt that the budget bills had been kept under control.

Wade was exultant. "The action on these bills has been good for the state, and my work on them will go far toward creating a good image for me. Before long, I'll be able to announce my candidacy and feel that I have an excellent chance to win."

Kaye said, "I'm so proud of you, Wade. The papers this morning were very good to you. Even our 'worthy opponents' had positive things to say about you, if not about your bills."

He smiled broadly. "How are you going to like living in Washington, honey, and being involved in political society?"

"Oh, I'll do just fine with your help."

"Well, you just might be living there as Mrs. Senator Hamilton."

"We've got to get the marriage license first, dear," she chided him gently. "And to do that, we have to set a date. The future Mrs. Hamilton needs to plan a wedding with the future Senator Hamilton."

"Yes, I'm as anxious to set a date as you are. But I'm afraid I'm going to have to ask you to wait another week or so."

"What on earth for?" Kaye asked in surprise. "Has something happened you haven't mentioned?"

"This morning Dad told me our contract in Hong Kong is hanging in the balance. The owners seem about ready to renege on their agreement. Dad asked me to fly to Hong Kong tonight to see what I can do from that vantage point. Getting that firm's business can mean a great deal to our operations, as you know."

"You're leaving tonight?"

"Yes. Sorry, honey."

"Well, why can't we set the date right now so I can get started on plans?"

"I think it would be better if I could have a little time to go through my calendar plus check out political activities that would have to be considered."

Kaye sighed in disappointment, but gave him a smile.

He took her hands. "I just want to be sure that nothing can interfere with the wedding, and I don't want our honeymoon trip interrupted."

"Sure. I understand."

"I'll call you every day."

"I haven't told you what I did Friday night, and what I found out," said Kaye brightly as the waiter brought their desserts.

"You said something about going with a new-found friend to look for your ancestors or something. I was so busy I really didn't pay much attention."

"I know you didn't. You've repeatedly ignored me or changed the subject."

"Sorry, love."

Kaye then recounted her experience with Jan at the branch genealogy library. With enthusiasm, she told Wade about finding the Cook family and William Button, and then of the plans to search further. But Wade obviously didn't share her enthusiasm. He didn't even seem to be listening; seemed to be concentrating more on his dessert.

"We went to Jan's apartment after we left the library," Kaye continued, hoping to gain Wade's full attention. "I asked her to tell me what caused her interest in ancestors, thinking that might help me to understand my own interest."

"Oh."

"She said that her interest involves her religion." Quickly, Kaye added, "She's a Mormon."

Wade looked up, frowning. "Kaye, I wish you wouldn't get involved with the Mormons."

Startled, Kaye asked, "Why?"

"Oh, they're a strange . . . bunch. I'd just rather you didn't get friendly with them," he said.

"What do you know about the Mormons that bothers you so? What makes you think they're so strange? I found Jan to be very nice!"

"I've got to catch that plane." Kaye could see that to pursue her questions would do no good now. Wade stood. "Come on. Let's go."

At the airport, Kaye saw Wade off even though she was miffed at his treatment, but she sensed that to discuss the matter further would be useless at the moment. She went home and began to write the letters she and Jan had determined were necessary to continue her search.

Kaye couldn't decide what was bothering Wade. She was puzzled and angry by his abrupt and insensitive treatment. Yet she loved him enough to believe they could clear up the problem on his return. And she was not going to give up a friendship with Jan, who was kind to her, without knowing why.

In fact, Jan's explanation at the apartment continued to be with her. Whether the explanation was correct Kaye didn't know, but she could find no fault with it. Kaye had a list of several Bible references Jan had given her, and now she decided to look in her Bible and see what the scriptures really did say. Kaye was not a regular church attender but she did have a small white Bible given to her at her first communion. As a child, she had been taught about Jesus. She was certainly not adverse to religious ideas.

She found her Bible and read the passages. They were just as Jan had said, and she could find no quarrel with them as far as she could understand them.

A couple of days later, missing Wade, Kaye went again to the cafeteria, hoping to see Jan.

I really should have called her to have lunch with me, Kaye thought. But a moment later Jan walked in and Kaye beckoned to her.

"It's good to see you again, Jan. Wade is out of the country and I'm alone. Won't you share my table?"

"Thanks, Kaye, I'd be happy to join you."

"Wade went to Hong Kong on business a couple of days ago and won't be back for a while," Kaye repeated.

"Did you tell him about our find before he left?"

"Yes, but I'm afraid he's not interested."

Jan shrugged. "Some people are and some aren't."

They chatted for a few moments, then Kaye said, "I wrote to the county clerk the other day, as you suggested. There hasn't been time yet for a response."

"Sometimes the clerks take so long you wonder if they ever will respond, but they usually do."

"I also looked up those scriptural references you gave me," Kaye continued. "I could find no problem with them. In fact, the subject interests me. Do you have anything more I could read?"

Jan looked startled. "As a matter of fact, I have. I had a few copies of the Book of Mormon at home I was planning to take to the church Sunday. When I opened my briefcase this morning, I found one copy in with my papers. This Book of Mormon may not be what you had in mind, but if you want the book it's yours."

Kaye remembered Wade's warning about the Mormons. But she could still see no reason for his negative attitude.

"What is the Book of Mormon?" she asked. "I've heard it's your Bible but you obviously use the Bible, too, or you wouldn't have given me the references you did."

"The Book of Mormon is not a discourse on genealogy or temple marriage, but it should answer questions for you." Jan explained, "Actually the book is a history of people who lived on this continent from about 600 B.C. to 420 A.D. and of the visit of Christ to them after his resurrection. We consider the Book of Mormon to be a companion scripture to the Bible."

Now it was Kaye's turn to be startled. "Christ on this continent? Can you prove that from the Bible?"

"You might consider the Gospel of John where Christ tells the people that he will go to his other sheep not of that fold, or in other words, people not of that country. He told the Book of Mormon people they were those people."

This is all too strange, thought Kaye. Maybe Wade was right. Yet she heard herself say, "With Wade gone, I do have some time on my hands. Reading the book might be interesting."

At least, she thought, I can't be hurt by reading it.

"Okay," said Jan, "I'll send the book upstairs to you this afternoon. Oh, by the way, before you begin, turn to about the next to the last page and read verses 4 and 5 of chapter 10. I'll see if I can find you some literature on genealogy, too, since you've asked."

That evening Kaye sat down and picked up the book Jan had given her. Then she laid it down again. Wade didn't want her to get involved with the Mormons and she didn't want to displease him. But how could she possibly be hurt by reading a book? She felt she had enough intelligence to determine most of the time what was of value and what should be discarded.

She couldn't see anything about Jan being a Mormon that would cause any concern. In fact, the opposite was true. Jan was a very nice person. Kaye looked long and hard at the book on the coffee table. She decided she would worry about settling the problem with Wade later. She could only hope he would understand. She picked up the book.

Kaye remembered Jan's suggestion that she read certain verses at the end of the book and she turned to them. So I must pray, she thought as she read, if I'm to find out if the book is true. That's a reasonable suggestion. If the book isn't true, I want to know, and if it is . . . I guess I must find out.

After considering for some moments what she should say, with embarrassment because she didn't pray often, Kaye knelt. Her words were few. They didn't come easily, but when she finished her prayer, Kaye had a feeling of satisfaction that she had done something good. Then she began to read.

In three evenings, Kaye Button read the Book of Mormon. She followed the advice of the last verses, at first fearing to know whether the book was true but not daring not to read to find out. As she read, she felt a familiar spirit such as was mentioned in the Bible, and an increased enthusiasm.

With the book completed, she knew she must take the final test, and again she knelt down. With all her heart she pleaded to know if the book was true, and she arose from her knees with warmth and joy, and with an assurance that it was, indeed, the word of the Lord. She wept.

"I want to know more," Kaye told her friend, Jan, the next day in the cafeteria.

"I'll help you," responded Jan. "I have found a few brochures and articles on the subjects you asked about."

"Oh, thanks. I'm anxious to see them."

Jan smiled. Her eyes held an extra sparkle. "Would you like to go to church with Jimmy and me Sunday?"

Kaye felt hesitant, but she agreed.

On the day following Kaye's conversation with Jan, Wade called her from Hong Kong.

"I just about had the contract all wrapped up," he told Kaye, "when a fire broke out in the factory that was to produce the contracted merchandise. The building is badly damaged."

"Oh, that's terrible! I hope you weren't hurt," Kaye responded.

"No. I wasn't even there at the time." Wade then described the fire and the damage to the building.

"What happens now? Are you coming home?"

"Not just yet. The ashes are hardly cold, but Dad is going to take up the fire with the Board and see if, rather than having me just come home, we can buy out the factory—rebuild it ourselves."

"I haven't seen your dad this morning so he hasn't told me."

"If the Board approves, and I think they will, I believe that will ultimately be better for the company than the old contract would have been. At any rate, I'll be staying here for a while—maybe another month or six weeks—until we get this taken care of."

"If it must be," she said, disappointed.

"Honey, I miss you and I'll get back as soon as I can."

Kaye sighed. More delay. Then her eye caught a note on her desk. "Oh, before I forget, you know that man in Kansas City—can't think of his name right now—the one you wanted to head up your campaign there when you start?"

"Yes?"

"He contacted me to report that he's sold his business as you directed so there'll be no conflict of interest. He's ready to go."

"I've changed my mind about him. Tell Dad to get rid of him. I've found someone I like better for the job."

"But," protested Kaye, "he's already sold his business!"

"Can't help that. I've got to have people who can help me win. I'm not sure he can. He's got powerful enemies I didn't know about before who could hurt me. I'll tell you when I get back. Dad will pay him off."

Stifling her feelings of unease about Wade's comment, Kaye said, "I have something to tell you when you get back."

"Can you tell me now?"

"I'd rather tell you when you're here. It'll keep."

Kaye was sure that her experiences would be better told in person than on the phone, or even by mail. She noted again that Wade had not once, in their conversation, mentioned her new interest in genealogy.

Chapter Eleven

Since Janice Connors was a person who believed that life was meant to be enjoyed, she was always able to find something to be enthusiastic about. A regular Pollyanna, Jimmy Halvorsen, Jan's fiance, called her, but she protested.

"I read that book about Pollyanna when I was little," she laughed, "but she was too sweet, a bit saccharine, for me. I must have a mischievous streak in me she didn't have."

It was true that Jan had a happy outlook. And few things gave her more delight than to talk about, and be involved in, her church. She took advantage of various opportunities given her to learn and to grow, and when she began to be interested in her ancestry, no one who knew her was surprised that she would develop great enthusiasm for that, too.

Jan had seen Kaye—a girl she considered to be beautiful and sophisticated—a few times before they met in the elevator. She was surprised when Kaye asked to join her at her table because she didn't consider herself in the same class with such a sophisticated person. Always glad to talk about the church and about genealogy, however, she welcomed Kaye's questions, even though she didn't expect her questions to be based on anything more then superficial curiosity.

She was even more surprised when, several days later, Kaye called to ask more questions. But Jan certainly did not intend to lose an opportunity to encourage someone else's interest in genealogy—which was why she had invited Kaye to go to the library. There were even more surprises for Jan— Kaye's interest in why genealogy mattered and her request for more materials to read. Looking back, Jan knew she hadn't put that Book of Mormon in her briefcase by accident, yet the book was there when Kaye asked for literature. And now Kaye had agreed to attend church.

Did Jan dare suggest to Kaye that she have missionaries call? She wanted her new friend to share the joy she knew but she didn't want to go too fast and to risk driving her away. So Jan tried to keep her enthusiasm in check, to let Kaye set her own pace. Jan would see what Sunday brought. Perhaps she could tell what she should do then. She'd discuss the situation with Jimmy.

As for Kaye, she had a desire to know something about almost everything. This desire, she decided, was what drew her to talk to Jan about genealogy. But learning more about the subject, Kaye saw that its appeal lay very much in the strength of the family. Her own family—father, mother, older brother, Roland, now married, and younger sister, Kippy—had a close relationship. Except for the letter to her father about Great-grandfather Button, however, Kaye had not said much about her research efforts nor that Jan was a Mormon. Kaye wanted to find some exciting information first, to illustrate her interest and effort.

But to take the Book of Mormon when Wade had expressly requested her not to get involved made Kaye feel uneasy. She respected his intelligence, knowledge and usually very good judgment. And he normally respected her interests and opinions. In fact, the mutual appreciation they shared for each other's mental capacities was a strong bond in their relationship. Kaye normally wouldn't oppose his request, but Wade had never before been so antagonistic. Kaye could hardly believe he would refuse even to discuss the subject.

Then there was the matter of the prayer Kaye had offered. When was the last time she had really prayed? There was an inexplicable something that drew her on. And she knew she had received an answer to her prayer: The Book of Mormon was unquestionably true.

Kaye was not looking for a new church. Oh, she had her first communion when she was young, and she believed in God, but attending church was something reserved for Christmas and a few other occasions. So it was with a curiosity and reluctance mixed with mysterious pull that caused Kaye to accept Jan's invitation to attend church with her and Jimmy. Kaye wanted to find out for herself what went on so that she could tell Wade when he got home.

The first thing Kaye noticed as she walked into the foyer of the building with Jan and Jimmy was a lot of people visiting with a lot of other people. Everyone was shaking hands, patting shoulders and chatting—quite a contrast to the quiet, solemn atmosphere she was used to in her own church. Jan introduced her to a man she called Bishop Harvey. Bishop Harvey, Jan told Kaye, was the chief officer of the congregation, or ward, as they called it. He was attired not in vestments but in a business suit. He was not tall and he was slightly overweight, with hair thinning on top. But the man had a warm smile, a firm handclasp, and he appeared to Kaye to be genuinely pleased to see her.

Jan and Jimmy introduced Kaye to several other people, and then they went to a room where, Jan explained, a Sunday School class was held. A young man, with the help of numerous visual aids, presented a lesson on Jonah. An animated discussion followed, and Kaye enjoyed the class very much.

Why doesn't Wade want me to have anything to do with the Mormons? she wondered. What is he afraid of?

The class over, they went into the chapel and took their seats. The room was nice but simple. It contained rows of benches with hymnals in racks on the back of each. At the front of the room was a pulpit on a platform with a row of seats behind it. Choir members were seated behind this row of seats. Kaye saw Bishop Harvey standing behind the pulpit.

"This meeting is what we call Sacrament Meeting," whispered Jimmy. "It's comparable to your worship service."

First, the congregation sang a hymn. Kaye enjoyed listening to Jimmy with his fine baritone voice. She could see why Jan loved him. Jimmy appeared to have the same enthusiasm for life that Jan did. They held hands and exchanged tender glances.

Kaye then observed three young men seated behind a table set at one side at the front of the chapel. Several younger boys sat facing them on the other side of the table. Items on the table were covered with a white cloth.

"What is that for?" Kaye whispered.

"The Sacrament of the Lord's Supper—bread to be broken and individual cups of water," Jan explained quietly.

Following the invocation and another hymn, a prayer was said by one of the young men at the table, and the younger boys started down the aisles. Each carried a silver tray containing the broken bread. Kaye reached for her purse for money, but Jan stopped her.

"No," she whispered, shaking her head.

"But I want to contribute," Kaye whispered back.

"We don't have collection plates. I'll explain after meeting."

The bishop again stood at the pulpit. But instead of preaching himself, which Kaye expected him to do, the bishop introduced other speakers, apparently lay members of the congregation, which gave Kaye even more questions to ask.

Then an abrupt movement caught Kaye's attention. Across the aisle and a row ahead of her, two big brown eyes peered at her over the top of a bench. Kaye winked, and the little head dropped down. In a few seconds the whole face, topped with curly dark hair, appeared, and a small boy, who looked to be about two years old, gave Kaye a wide grin. Suddenly, with obvious shyness, the tot buried his face against the chest of the man who held him.

A girl about four or five years old, who sat by them, turned to look at Kaye. She had blue eyes, and a face framed by long hair that curled slightly at the ends. The man must be their father, thought Kaye. There's such a strong family resemblance. I wonder if the mother is that pretty? She could not see a woman sitting nearby that could be the mother of the two children.

The choir began to sing, bringing Kaye back to the service. A woman gave a talk. Kaye listened intently. Many things that were said were familiar to her but some ideas expressed were not. She would have to ask Jan about them.

When the meeting was over, Jimmy asked, "Any questions?"

"Yes, a lot," Kaye replied.

"Well, fire away. I'll see if I can answer them."

"Not on an empty stomach," Jan interrupted. "Let's go to my house first for dinner."

"I'll go for that," said Jimmy. To Kaye he added, "This girl of mine is a great cook."

Kaye agreed. "Yes, I've been to her apartment."

While they were eating, Kaye asked about the children she had seen at church.

"Oh, you must mean Tessa and Darby," said Jan. "Aren't they beautiful? They're Corey Hollister's children."

"Where was their mother? She must be a beauty, too."

"She was. She died about six months ago. She got sick suddenly and was gone in a matter of days. There was nothing doctors could do." Jan stood up. "Who would like ice cream?"

After dinner, they sat in the living room. The questions and answers began. First, Jimmy explained to Kaye about administering the Sacrament of the Lord's Supper. Next, Kaye asked about the collection plate, or rather the lack of one.

"We have no paid clergy," Jimmy explained. "Our bishop owns a hardware store. The Sunday School teacher, on weekends, is a jet pilot with the National Guard."

"How does your church meet financial obligations?"

"With tithing," said Jimmy. "We are expected to pay a tenth of our income." After several more questions, Jimmy paused. "This is a rather hit-and-miss approach to doctrines of our church, Kaye. Would you like to have missionaries come to explain? They're trained for this service."

For a moment Kaye was silent. So this was what her adventure was coming to! She was not surprised, but what would Wade have to say about the introduction of missionaries? So far, she had not found anything he could realistically object to. What if she could find no problems with what missionaries might tell her? Kaye wasn't ready to change her religion. Still there was the Book of Mormon. And because of her prayer, Kaye knew the book was true. That experience had touched her deeply, but she hadn't told Wade about it. She hadn't yet determined what to tell him, how to tell him, or even if she should tell him anything.

Finally, she spoke. "I'm not interested in becoming a Mormon. For one thing, Wade would object." She hesitated. "But I would like to learn more."

"Of course," Jan said, "we don't want to cause conflict between you and Wade."

"I don't want missionaries to visit me," Kaye continued, "but I would be willing to have you two tell me what I want to know—if that's all right."

"It's a deal," said Jimmy. "But let me be honest with you. I've been a missionary myself. Many young people in the church, when they are about nineteen years old, spend a year and a half as missionaries at their own expense. I served in California, although many of our missionaries serve overseas."

"I'm trapped," said a surprised and amused Kaye, "but I'm making no promises, and I do have Wade's opposition to worry about."

"Don't let us make you feel trapped, Kaye. You will never be asked to do anything against your will. When you say 'stop,' we'll stop."

"Fair enough."

"Okay," said Jimmy. "When would you like to begin?"

Chapter Twelve

When Kaye first attended the Mormon Church with Jan and Jimmy, Wade had been in Hong Kong for two weeks. He called Kaye frequently to report on progress in rebuilding the factory and to give her instructions for the management of the office during his extended absence. Once Kaye tried to tell him about her new interest in genealogy, and about attending a Mormon Church service, but he cut her short.

"Kaye, I asked you not to get involved with these people." His voice revealed his irritation. "It can only lead to grief."

"I haven't found one thing yet that could make you feel that way, honey," she responded. "Can't we talk about it when you get home?"

"It looks like we'll need to. Please, dear, don't do something you'll regret, or that will jeopardize my chances for congress. I've let nothing get in my way so far, and I'll do anything I have to to get there. Anything!"

"All right. I love you."

"Love you, too."

Kaye's next meeting with Jan and Jimmy was not just a hit-and-miss question-and-answer session. Nor were any of their subsequent meetings. Although Kaye had seen the name of Joseph Smith on the title page of the Book of Mormon, she now heard, for the first time, of his search for a church he could join. She was quiet and thoughtful as Jimmy recounted how God the Father and his Son, Jesus Christ, appeared in person to the young boy and told him not to join any church.

"I knew that Brigham Young headed the Mormons and led them to Utah," she said, "but, to be perfectly honest, I didn't know much else, nor really cared."

"What we tell you is true," added Jan, "every word. I'll give you a copy of Joseph Smith's story in his own words for you to take home."

"But how could he see God when God is a spirit? An—an essence? And Christ is a part of God, a physical manifestation of him."

"There are lots of scriptures that say otherwise." Jimmy said, "Let's turn to the account of Christ's baptism. You see here that John was baptizing Jesus, yet the Father's voice came from heaven. Also Stephen, the martyr, saw the Son standing on the right hand of the Father. And there are other scriptures that show this principle. I'll give you some to check out."

Kaye felt dubious, but she let him continue. Maybe Wade's right about the Mormons after all, she thought.

She wondered at Jimmy's words, too, when he explained that the church that Christ had organized during his ministry in the Holy Land was based on a foundation of apostles and prophets holding the authority to act and to receive continual revelation. But it had vanished from the earth in less than three hundred years.

"The church had gone into a state of apostasy," Jimmy explained.

"Apostasy?"

"Yes, not an unusual occurence except in its duration. Apostasy happened all through the Old Testament—at the time of Enoch, Noah, a classic example, and all through the period of the kings of Israel and Judah. And you read about apostasy numerous times in the Book of Mormon account of that people."

"And you're telling me apostasy happened again after the New Testament, I take it," Kaye surmised.

"Yes," he responded. "All through the New Testament the apostles taught that this would happen, and, in Acts 3:19-21, Peter specifically states that Christ's second coming would not occur until there should be a falling away and a restoration."

"Now you want me to believe that your Joseph Smith was told that that apostasy was in effect, and I guess he was the one who was supposed to make changes."

"Yes, you're right on target," said Jan. "He was the one designated to restore the church to be based on apostles and prophets, direct authority from the Lord, and continual revelation."

"And he did just that," added Jimmy. "But we'd better not get into anything more today. You've got a lot to think about already."

"You're asking me to take your word on many things," Kaye commented.

"Correction, Kaye." Jimmy smiled. "Don't take our word for one bit of what we've told you. Study, then ask the Lord."

*   *   *

"Let us give you a chance to see us when we let our hair down," explained Jan later as she invited Kaye to a church picnic. "Our ward—that's our congregation—is going to the park for a barbecue. If you like good food, please come."

"Oh, I wish Wade were here," said Kaye after she had accepted the invitation. "It might break down his negative feelings."

The evening of the barbecue was warm—perfect weather for an outing. As Kaye, Jan and Jimmy arrived, they were greeted by many of the people Kaye had seen at the church. Bishop Harvey, wearing a chef's hat and apron, was supervising the barbecue. Others were working alongside him. Children were running and laughing as two or three young women tried to organize activities for them. A group of teen-agers were playing a fast game of volleyball, while others were involved in a softball game.

Near the barbecue were two banquet tables loaded with cakes, salads, sliced ripe tomatoes, rolls and butter, and soft-drink dispensers holding rootbeer and orange. Tubs filled with ice and watermelons were nearby. Kaye and Jan added their salads to the collection, and Jimmy went to join a second volleyball team that was forming.

As Corey Hollister, the young man Kaye had seen at church, came by with his children, Tessa and Darby, in tow, Tessa's young friends called and she ran to join them, her ponytail bobbing, Darby following not far behind.

"Corey," Jan called, "come meet my friend, Kaye."

Corey came over and Jan introduced him to Kaye. He extended his hand. "I'm glad to meet you, Kaye. Are you new in the ward?"

"Oh, I'm not a Mormon," Kaye hastily explained. "Jan and I are good friends. We work in the same building downtown."

"Well, I'm glad you could join us tonight. Hope you have a nice time. Now if you'll excuse me, I'll join the ballgame." He gave the girls a friendly smile and trotted off to join Jimmy.

The evening passed all too quickly. After the ball games were over, the group ate. Following the meal, teen-agers presented a program. It was purely amateur, punctuated with laughter and hi-jinks. Kaye was having a grand time, but she wished that Wade were there, too.

Finally, people began gathering up dishes and children, and moving toward their cars. The leaving was as gradual as the arriving had been. A few of the younger folks began another volleyball game. Kaye and Jan began sorting out their dishes from others on the tables when a shriek suddenly pierced the air. Kaye and Jan turned just in time to see Darby Hollister balanced on his stomach on the edge of a tub that had held watermelons. As he reached for a chunk of ice he teetered forward and went head first into the water.

Kaye was nearest the tub. In two steps she was able to grab the sputtering, gasping youngster by the waistband of his pants to pull him out. She held the child in her arms and comforted him until Corey ran up.

Thank you for rescuing my son," said Corey, taking the child.

"Oh, he's in trouble again," added a disgusted Tessa.

"He's all right," Kaye answered, "Just frightened."

"But look at you. You're all wet." Corey told Kaye, "I'll pay to have your outfit cleaned."

"That's okay. The water won't hurt it."

"I got wet, Daddy," interjected Darby, water still running out of his plastered-down curls.

"Yes, we'll have to get you home and into a hot tub," said his father. And to Kaye, "Thank you again." With Darby on his arm and Tessa by the hand, he left.

"He does a great job with those children," Jan commented to Kaye as she and Jimmy walked with her to the car. Corey's mother takes them during the day but he has them with him as much as possible otherwise."

Kaye continued meeting with Jan and Jimmy to discuss the doctrines of the LDS Church, sometimes at her apartment and sometimes at Jan's. After discussing a principle or doctrine, Jimmy would give her references to check and literature to read. Often Kaye studied in the evenings. At other times she read during breaks and lunch at work.

She was amazed at some of the doctrines and principles she was learning. There was more to Mormonism, she discovered, than abstinence from alcohol, tobacco and coffee, which she, as a non-Mormon, knew most about Mormons. She began to discover that there was, indeed, ample scriptural proof for the numerous doctrines Jan and Jimmy explained to her. She was surprised by the number of prophecies in both the Old and the New Testaments and in the Book of Mormon about the apostasy of the church organized by Christ and of the restoration in latter times.

"I guess you might say that's it in a nutshell," Jimmy said one night. "Either the church continued from the time of Christ or it didn't. It couldn't go both ways. If the church Christ organized did continue, the spin-offs from that church are wrong because they were cut off from it. If the church didn't continue, those who protested are still wrong because their mother church had apostatized. Thus Joseph Smith and the restoration had to be."

Kaye didn't answer. She had realized that her discussions with her friends might come to this, but somehow she hadn't anticipated the conflict it would bring. First, there was Wade. What would this knowledge do to her marriage plans? Surely, when she had a chance to talk to Wade they would be able to solve this difficulty. She refused to consider the alternatives at this point.

Kaye had not yet said anything to her family about her interest in the Mormon Church. Oh, she'd told them about Jan and Jimmy, the ward picnic, rescuing Darby from the tub, her efforts to locate Great-grandfather Button. The response was rather indifferent.

Of course, she herself had asked about the Mormons merely out of curiosity. With that curiosity satisfied, she could just drop the subject and continue to be friends with Jan and Jimmy. They had promised no pressure, and in time she was sure Wade would accept them as friends, too. Anyway,

Wade was sure to be elected to Congress in another year, which meant they'd be living in Washington, D.C.

Jan's voice interrupted her thoughts. "Do the things we've taught disturb you?"

"Perhaps some," she replied. "I guess I'm concerned as much as anything by how I'm afraid Wade will react."

"Trust in the Lord to help you," said Jan.

"Perhaps I shouldn't continue this. You promised no pressure," Kaye reminded them.

"Yes, we promised, and we'll keep our promise. But would you consider just one more get-together? We'd like to explain about how we know who we are, where we came from, why we're here and what the prospects are for life after this life. This subject's the best part."

"You mean there are places besides heaven or hell?"

"Oh, most definitely!"

"And what do you mean, 'where we came from'?" Kaye grasped this statement quickly.

"Let's save that until next time."

"It has something to do with genealogy, doesn't it, you sly fox." Kaye laughed. "Okay, one more meeting."

"Remember," added Jimmy, his tone serious, "pray about what you've heard. You've got to find out for yourself, not just take our word."

Find out for yourself, Kaye thought later that evening. I've been trying. I have read and studied all the scriptures and other literature they have given me. We've prayed together each meeting, sometimes with me doing the praying lately. She sighed and leaned back in her chair. I'll have just one more meeting with them and call it quits as far as meetings go.

The phone interrupted her thoughts. Kaye picked it up. "Hello?"

"Hello, darling, it's Wade. I've been trying to reach you. Where have you been?"

"I just spent the evening with Jan and Jimmy. I'm sorry I missed you."

"I just wanted to tell you I'm leaving for home tomorrow. The job has reached a point where I can leave it now—sooner than I had expected—and I must get back to my work at home."

Kaye's heart pounded. "Oh, honey, I'll be glad to see you. When will you get here?"

"The plane lands at 6:10 day after tomorrow, your time, of course. Meet me at the airport and we'll go to dinner."

"I'll be there!"

Day after tomorrow! He'll be here in two days! Kaye was ecstatic, but then she paused. Two days, and we'll have to talk about our problem. She sensed that the talk might not be pleasant.

Kaye was at the airport as planned, and any thought of disharmony between them was forgotten as he caught her in his arms. They talked as they walked to the car, all through dinner at the club and driving home afterward. There was so much to get caught up on. Eventually, Kaye told Wade about going to the ward picnic with Jan and Jimmy.

"You were at a Mormon party?" he asked, with annoyance.

"Yes. It was just a simple picnic in the park. I wish you could have been there, too. You know how you love barbecued beef. It was excellent."

"Kaye, I thought I told you not to have anything more to do with those Mormons."

"I can't see why you object. They're nice people. They've been very friendly with me. Helped fill up the lonesome hours while you were gone."

"Oh, I know all about the Mormons, and I don't want you associating with them. They can do you no good, and they certainly won't help my career."

"Your career!" Kaye exclaimed. "They're voters, the same as the rest of us. How could they possibly hurt?" She was immediately sorry for her outburst. Angry words wouldn't solve the problem.

"Honey," she added more softly, "I'm going to Jan's Thursday night, and Jimmy will be there. Will you come? Please?"

"No, and I'll ask you again not to see them. Tell them you can't make it."

"I can't do that and I don't want to. I wish you would reconsider. You might find the Mormons aren't as bad as you think."

"I said no, and I expect you to cancel your engagement." Wade's knuckles were white on the steering wheel, his mouth a firm line.

"Please tell me, Wade," Kaye implored, "what do you know that's so awful?"

Wade refused to answer the question, as he repeated his request that she not go to Jan's.

Kaye was stunned. She had expected unpleasantness from Wade but she had not anticipated his bitterness, over what, she didn't know. She was aware that Wade could be forceful, even overpowering at times, which worked to his advantage in the General Assembly when a situation required it, but she had never seen this side of him. Wade had always been kind and tender with her. But she didn't feel it was fair of him to ask her to give up her friends, especially when he gave no good reason for it.

They drove to her apartment building. Wade leaned across her to open the door.

"Good night, Kaye," he said coolly.

"Good night, dear. I'll see you in the morning." It was the first time he had not shown her the courtesy of seeing her to the door. He didn't kiss her nor even thank her for bringing his car to the airport. Kaye was angry and upset with Wade's cool behavior, but she decided to say nothing. Angry words spoken now would only make discussion harder later. Perhaps when he'd had a good night's sleep and a chance to get over jet lag, they could talk calmly. She watched him drive away, wondering what to expect in the morning and what to tell Jan and Jimmy.

Chapter Thirteen

The atmosphere at the office next morning was not quite normal, but Kaye tried to act as though the unpleasantness of the night before had not happened. She came early to have Wade's desk ready. When he arrived, he gave her a peck on the cheek. With a casual, "Good morning," he went in his office. Kaye watched him go, wondering what he would do.

The day was busy with the catching up Wade had to do, and he said nothing of his angry words of the previous evening. Nothing, that is, until the rest of the staff were leaving at the end of the day.

He walked out of his office and to Kaye's desk. She looked up from clearing away papers and covering her typewriter.

"It's good to have you back. You must be tired after such a long day," she said.

"Yes," he replied, "it is good. Listen, about last night, I'm sorry to have lost my temper. Jet lag, I guess."

"That's okay."

"I should have realized," he continued, "that this thing of yours with those people is just a passing fancy, a phase."

Kaye raised her eyebrows. A phase! she thought, as though I were a child. But she said nothing.

"Mother asked me to bring you home to dinner tonight. Okay?"

"Yes, Wade, that would be fine. I haven't seen your folks for awhile."

"And tomorrow night I'll get tickets for the Broadway road company that's opening. Then we need to talk about setting a wedding date."

Kaye shoved a handful of papers in her desk and picked up her purse. "We need to talk about a date, but I can't tomorrow. I have an appointment. I told you about it. Another night?"

Wade scowled. "All right. Let's go."

The evening was a bit strained, although Kaye could see that Wade and his parents tried to be cordial. It was obvious to Kaye that some of the conversation of the night before Wade had discussed with the senior Hamiltons. And, judging from the atmosphere, she felt sure that their feelings were the same as their son's.

Kaye was glad to go home. She was troubled by the whole situation. Wade might well be trying to maneuver her into a position where she would have to choose between him and her new interest. If she had to choose, which would it be?

When Wade was not in the office the next day, Kaye was glad. He had several political meetings to attend, and she wasn't sure whether he had planned the meetings to avoid her and not be around until after her meeting that night. Whichever way, she was relieved.

Why, she wondered, did it matter so much to him that she should have developed an interest in a particular church? And perhaps, on the other side of the coin, why did it matter so much to her to continue her interest in that particular church? She didn't seriously feel that this interest would endanger her marriage, but certainly the problem would have to be cleared up first. Maybe tonight's session with her friends would provide some answers.

Driving to Jan's apartment, Kaye marveled at the changes that had occurred in her life recently. A couple of months ago, she would have laughed had someone told her how deeply she would become involved in religion, especially the Mormon religion, and about an interest in people who had lived well over a hundred years earlier: Kaye, the sophisticate. Kaye, on her way to becoming a senator's wife. Kaye, the ambitious business woman.

But why should what she was change just because she had read the Book of Mormon? Even if she were to join that church, her goals shouldn't have to be given up, should they? There! Now she had put in conscious thought what had begun to form cautiously in her mind, but pushed hastily aside. If she were to join the church . . .

True to his word, Jimmy had not badgered her nor forced ideas upon her. Kaye felt that she simply wanted to know about the Mormon Church because she was always seeking new information. But the answer to one of her questions invariably led to several more. And Jimmy had answers that made more sense to her than any she had ever heard before.

For example, he had explained to her the transgression and fall of Adam not as a sexual sin casting shame on all mankind, but the eating of a substance that made him subject to death, a necessary step that only he was responsible for. That, then, had brought up the need for Christ and his mission, to atone for the fall and for all our sins, pending repentance, and make possible the resurrection. These Mormon doctrines gave her an entirely new outlook on religion. If only she could get Wade to see this!

Kaye told her friends that Wade had returned and that he had not been keen on having her continue their discussions, but she didn't yet feel like she needed to tell Jan and Jimmy how strongly Wade felt.

"I had hoped that he would be interested in what I am interested in," she said, "at least enough to have a casual acquaintance with it."

"I wish there were some way we could help you," Jan said sympathetically.

"He won't even agree to meet you."

"I guess you just have to remember, Kaye," said Jimmy, "that the Lord moves in mysterious ways his wonders to perform. Not much comfort to you right now, I'm sure. But keep it in mind. Have faith."

They turned to the discussion, and Jimmy gave her another new idea. He told of a spirit world in which all mortals lived as spirit persons, the sons and daughters of God the Father; the necessity of these persons coming to the earth to take mortal bodies to school their spirits, to be tried and tested away from the presence of the Father; a spirit world after death where the gospel is taught to those denied the chance as mortals; and of resurrection for all to whatever reward or punishment each merited.

"Christ said there were many mansions in his Father's house," Jimmy explained.

"And the highest reward, the greatest 'mansion,' " added Jan, "is to return to the presence of our Father in Heaven, sealed for the eternities to our companion and family."

When Jimmy finished his explanation, Kaye sat silently. She felt warm, peaceful and good with these two kind friends as they discussed these subjects. Oh, why couldn't she pursuade Wade to share her happy experience? Perhaps now it was time to share what she had learned with her parents and Kippy. She would write tonight.

Wade apparently felt the best way to handle the situation was to ignore it, that having granted Kaye one last visit to the Mormons, the episode would end.

Kaye wrote to her family and, in telling them of what she had learned, she came to realize that she had found a precious pearl, a pearl that offered a meaning and purpose to life that she had never before known. She knew The Church of Jesus Christ of Latter-day Saints, the doctrines it taught, and the authority it held was true.

Her heart was heavy, notwithstanding, because she loved Wade, yet he would not let her share the joy she had found. She decided to avoid the subject, thinking that perhaps time would soften him, hoping that a proper occasion would eventually present itself.

For several days, Kaye tried to act as though nothing had happened and Wade did not say anything more. But it soon became obvious that the issue would have to be met. The moment came as they were driving to a party at the club, given by his parents for a group of board members and other associates.

"You've been awfully quiet lately," he said. "Want to talk about it?"

"I guess we do need to settle this once and for all," she replied.

"The problem is the Mormons, isn't it?"

"I just don't understand your feelings toward them. You refuse to listen to anything, you won't meet my friends, and you won't tell me why. If I just knew why . . ."

His voice was calm. "The Mormons! I don't need *them!* I have everything a man could want. I come from a prominent family, have the best education. I'm successful in business, I'll be the president of the company some day—unless I become the president of the United States first, and maybe even then. I have practically everything I want that money can buy, and someday I'll have it all! I don't need the Mormons. I don't need any religion."

Why, you pompous prig! Kaye thought. Everything you have except your education could be wiped out overnight. For the first time she realized what Wade really was. She could see his selfish ambition, his lust for power.

Wade reached for her hand, "And I have a beautiful woman to marry. I picked carefully when I chose you, because a proper choice was essential to promote my career."

That statement startled Kaye. "I thought you wanted to marry me because you loved me."

"Oh, that, too," he replied offhandedly, "but a man in my position must have the right wife."

"And I was interested in Mormonism because it promised the possibility of marriage forever," she said under her breath.

"What was that?"

"Oh, nothing. But that still doesn't explain why you have such a violent reaction to the idea of meeting my friends, or even just letting me be interested in them."

They were driving past the park. Wade turned in and stopped the car. They got out and walked to a bench.

"Kaye, my darling," his mouth was grim now, his jaw firm in spite of his endearing term, "I have read about these people. There are books about them. The Mormons were driven out of this state because they were scum. Surely you must know what people say about Mormons, even now! Do you think I could afford, in my position, to have my wife interested in people like that?"

"Oh, Wade," she protested, releasing all the feelings she'd held back for so long, "they're just people! They're good, honest, hard-working people! What you have read was written by their enemies. Have you ever read the Book of Mormon to see what it really is? Have you ever studied their doctrines to see what they actually believe? Have you met any Mormons to see what they are really like?"

Wade's voice expressed amazement. "Kaye, what's gotten into you?"

She spoke firmly, no longer holding back. "I'll answer for you. No! You've done none of these things! You're satisfied to condemn without knowing."

When Wade didn't answer, Kaye continued. "I love you, Wade, and I want to share with you something I found that is good and beautiful, but you won't listen."

"Good and beautiful!" he exploded. "Kaye, I forbid you to have anything more to do with those Mormons!" He got up and paced around the bench.

"Wade," she said, softly enough that he turned toward her. "Wade," she repeated, "you can't dictate whom I shall have as my friends. I've always believed that I would do everything I could to become for you the best wife possible. I would never do anything to hurt you or your career. These friends wouldn't be hurtful, I promise."

"I forbid it," he repeated. "Do you hear me? I forbid it. I'll have what I want. Not you, not anyone nor anything else will stop me!"

"Then there's nothing more to say." Kaye fought back her tears, knowing that what he said was true. Remembering his tactics in the General Assembly and in business, she realized how he had used people to accomplish his own ends. She remembered the man in Kansas City, who had sold his business for Wade. And now Kaye could see that he was using even her. "You'd better get to your party. I'm going home." She stood up.

Wade caught her arm. "Kaye, don't make a scene. Get in the car."

Kaye pulled away from him. A taxi came down the street and she hailed it. As she climbed in, she looked back. She saw Wade standing where she left him, his shoulders drooping, watching as the taxi drove away. Typical of Wade, Kaye thought, was the way he gave a shrug and a toss of his head, got in his car and drove off. He'd go to the party, she knew, and put on a good show.

Arriving home, Kaye threw herself on her bed and sobbed, letting go all the tears she had forced herself to hold until that moment. Tonight she had seen a side of Wade she had not known. Somehow, somewhere, she had lost the man she loved. He no longer existed. The handsome, intelligent, leader of men, she now admitted, was ruthless and greedy for power. He was a narrow and calculating man who was unwilling to open his mind to any person or idea that was not in his plans.

But the biggest hurt of all for Kaye was the realization that Wade was willing to use her to reach his goals with no consideration for her needs and feelings. She was for Wade a means to an end, a property to be dictated to! Even married to him she wouldn't have been a wife, but a servant expected to do his bidding.

Hours passed before Kaye was able to sleep, and then she slept only fitfully. There was one thing she knew she had to do. Tomorrow she would write a letter of resignation from her job. She couldn't face going in to the office because she didn't want to explain her resignation to the staff nor face Wade. Wade would need no explanation. She would go home for a visit with her parents. Then she would begin looking for a new job.

Jimmy had said that the Lord moves in a mysterious way. Kaye hoped the Lord had something in mind for her.

Chapter Fourteen

As soon as she was able to make a reservation, Kaye flew to Chicago and home. With her letter of resignation in the mail, she had to get away from St. Louis, Wade and all the unpleasantness she'd had for a few days, and review her situation. Decisions needed to be made, and Kaye wanted to be away from distractions.

But if she had expected peaceful surroundings and comfort at home, her expectations were not met. Instead, she walked into another unhappy situation. Her letter had been received, and the response to her interest in Mormonism was anything but enthusiastic. The unpleasantness began at dinner that night as they were finishing dessert.

"How did you get involved with the Mormons anyway?" her father asked gruffly.

"I've told you," Kaye responded. "I met Jan, who is a Mormon, at the office, and we became friends while she helped me with genealogy. She was doing research and I got interested. You remember. I asked you about William Button."

"But I didn't know it was going to lead to this!" Mr. Button protested.

"I don't know what you mean by 'this,' " Kaye felt defensive again.

"Kaye, dear," her mother interjected, "it's just that those people are Mormons."

"There are a few Mormons at school," Kippy spoke up, "and they seem to be okay."

"Katherine," her mother spoke sharply, "don't be impertinent!"

Kippy shrugged. "One is student body president," she said. Kaye smiled, but quickly looked down to hide it. Her sixteen-year-old sister could always be counted on to come up with something unexpected.

The phone rang, and Kippy jumped up to answer. "It's probably for me," she said, and added over her shoulder as she flew out of the room, "or it might be a Mormon!"

Mr. Button choked on the water he was drinking, and Kaye smothered a laugh with a cough in her napkin.

Dinner finished, Kaye went with her parents to the living room.

"I'm sorry to have upset you," said Kaye. "I just wanted to share with you something I have found to be beautiful and special, and to ask you to meet my new friends."

"Oh, I know about the Mormons," her father stated. "They're such a peculiar people, and they have such strange beliefs. We've raised you to be a thinking and sensible person. I'm sorry to see you taken in."

Kaye decided to change the subject with her other news. "I've broken my engagement with Wade," she said. "That's why I came home. I need a change of scene."

"Oh, I'm so sorry, dear," her mother sympathized. "What ever happened?"

"I found out that Wade is not the man I believed him to be. He was more interested in what I could do for his career than he was in me as a person."

"Wade?" Mrs. Button was shocked. "I can hardly believe it!"

"Yes. To aspire to high positions, to have high goals, is one thing," Kaye explained, "but to want those goals for your own self-aggrandizement and to be willing to use anyone to reach them is quite another. I refused to be used. He didn't want me for me as much as for a means to help him achieve his ends. I'm not exactly homely, I'm not stupid, I come from a highly respected Chicago family. These things suited him just fine."

"Aren't you being a little hard on him?" asked Mr. Button. "He seemed like such a splendid person. You've just had a quarrel, and you're hurt."

"No, Dad, it's more than that. We did quarrel, and he did admit everything I told you. But I've had time to think since, and that quarrel only served to open my eyes to what should have already been apparent. I've begun to see how subtly he's been using and discarding people."

When neither parent spoke, Kaye continued. "I've quit my job. Naturally, I can't work for Wade any longer." Then, seeing her mother's distress, she added, "Mother, I wouldn't have been able to be my own person married to Wade. He wouldn't even have let me choose my own friends!"

"You mean the Mormons, don't you?" her father said bluntly.

"He forbade me to see them again. But even if he hadn't, I couldn't marry him because of what he is. He could achieve his goals honestly and without subterfuge, and be such a great man."

"Well, Kaye, I can accept that reason. You're an intelligent person and what you say could very well be true. But as to those Mormons, I'd rather that you didn't continue to associate with them. Regardless of Wade, I've never liked the Mormons. You're of age and can do as you wish, but I don't want those two you've spoken of or any others—or Mormonism at all—mentioned in this house again."

Kaye stayed in Chicago only one more day. Her heart ached to share with her family what she had learned and now knew to be true, but she realized that would have to wait. But getting a new job wouldn't wait, even though, with her qualifications, she didn't expect to have difficulty finding work. Also, she wanted to get back to Jan and Jimmy.

Most importantly, she had to decide whether to be baptized a Mormon. Her belief in Mormonism had already cost Kaye her marriage, subsequently her job, and, if she were to be baptized, might alienate her from her family. Would joining the church be worth the cost?

Upon returning to her apartment, Kaye found more discouraging news. Letters she had written in search of William Button were returning with little or no new information. Neither death certificate nor newspaper obituary she received mentioned his parents. The death certificate stated that he was born in Pennsylvania, but the town was not mentioned. Everyone heading west in those days, it seemed, must have gone through Pennsylvania on their way to somewhere else. Requests for information were so numerous that answers were rare, if at all, she was learning.

Following her first visit to the branch genealogy library with Jan, Kaye had gone back. Having found William Button as a child in the Oliver Cook family in Washington County, Ohio, Kaye had been spurred to check further records. She looked in the census index for Pennsylvania for 1860 and found Cooks in Westmoreland County where Uniontown was the county seat. In the small village of Cross Corners were the Oliver and Mollie Cook and one child she had found in the Ohio census. But there were no people with the surname of Button. Land deeds, tax records and other documents Kaye checked were also lacking Button names.

* * *

While Kaye was experiencing serious trials, Jan was enjoying one of the most beautiful and memorable occasions of her life: her wedding!

In August, Jimmy received his master's degree. Jan finished the last of the details for her reception, mailed the invitations, and packed her wedding dress. Then Jimmy and his parents and Jan with hers were off to Washington, D.C.

Jan's heart pounded as they approached the tall, stately temple towering above the trees. They could see it from some distance, and it seemed that the gold statue of Moroni on the highest spire was trumpeting the glad news, "Janice Connors is getting married today!" Hand in hand, Jan and Jimmy walked through the doors together.

When Jan walked into the small but elegant sealing room where they would speak their vows, Jimmy, dressed in white, was already there. He took her hand and squeezed it reassuringly. The room was beautiful, rich but simple in its decor. The chairs that lined the wall, the carpets and drapes were in soft colors. In the center of the room was the altar covered with tatted lace. Overhead was a glittering crystal chandelier. But perhaps the most striking feature of the room was the placement of two large perfect mirrors on opposite walls. The chandelier reflected in each as far as she could see.

John Clark, a temple worker and friend of the family, would be performing the ceremony. Dressed in white, he walked into the room and greeted them all. He invited the families and the few friends to be seated, and then he spoke of the marriage, the place it held in the gospel plan, and other topics of concern and of counsel to the young couple.

Jimmy and Jan knelt on opposite sides of the altar as the officiator stood at the head to begin the ceremony.

"Do you, James Martin Halvorsen, take Janice Elaine Connors . . ."

"Yes."

"Do you, Janice Elaine Connors, take James Martin Halvorsen . . ."

"Yes."

". . . husband and wife for time and for all eternity . . ."

Tears flowed freely and unashamedly as the officiator spoke. The ceremony completed, they kissed tenderly across the altar. Then they arose and Jimmy placed on her hand and she on his rings whose perfect circles symbolized the eternities; without beginning and without end. There were hugs and kisses and congratulations all around. Jan and Jimmy looked into the mirrors. Either way, the reflection was like their marriage, continuing into eternity. Jan was so happy she thought she would burst, and Jimmy's eyes said he felt the same way.

The newly married Halvorsens honeymooned in Florida for two weeks before returning to St. Louis for the reception. Kaye agreed to attend and to be responsible for the guest book. She enjoyed the assignment. Some of the people who came she had met at various times at church. Other faces were new to her.

Bishop Harvey and his wife walked in during the evening with Corey Hollister. They greeted Kaye cordially as they signed the book.

"Jimmy tells me he has given you the missionary discussions and that you are considering baptism, Kaye," said Bishop Harvey.

"I've been giving it some thought," she replied.

"Don't wait too long," Corey commented. "You have been told the truth, you know."

A short while later, Corey came back to where Kaye sat, carrying a plate of refreshments.

"Thought you might like something," he said.

"Thanks," she replied with a smile. "How are your children? I haven't seen them for a while."

"They're doing fine. Darby hasn't tried to drown himself more than twice since the time you pulled him out of the watermelon tub. Tessa is a good little scout. She helps her grandmother watch over her brother."

"Tessa is a beautiful child."

"Thank you. I understand that you work in the same building Jan does."

"I did, but I have a new job now with a contracting firm. It's some distance from here—the Palmer Towers, a new building a few blocks from the river on Allen Drive."

"I know the building. I designed it." He chuckled at her surprise. "I'm an architect. I work with Modern Architectural Design."

They were interrupted, then, by the arrival of more friends. Corey left, tossing almost lightly over his shoulder, "Don't wait too long for that baptism."

* * *

Two weeks later, Kaye was baptized. With many prayers and not a few tears, she decided that she must act on the conviction she had gained. Kaye was dressed in the white baptismal clothing provided, as Jan explained she would be. Also dressed in white, Jimmy took her by the hand and led her down into the font. Raising his arm to the square, he spoke the words of the prayer, and then gently lowered Kaye into the water and brought her up again. Afterward, dressed again in her street clothes but with her hair still damp, Jimmy and Bishop Harvey placed their hands on Kaye's head and confirmed her a member of The Church of Jesus Christ of Latter-day Saints. Kaye thought she had never been so happy.

* * *

On their return from their honeymoon trip, Jan and Jimmy had moved into a new apartment rented before they left. They hadn't completely furnished it, and Jan was like a child at Christmas as she looked for just the right furnishings.

"I want a room, this second bedroom, all in antique decor," she told Kaye one day shortly after Kaye's baptism. "I don't want to live in the past, so I'm just doing one room in antiques."

"Call it your genealogy room," Kaye suggested. "Those built-in shelves would be perfect for all your books and papers."

"Yes, plus what Jimmy has. And how about a big roll-top desk over here with a Tiffany lamp overhead?"

"A braided rug on the floor would brighten up the room."

"I'll get Jimmy and we can look for an old four-poster bed, and we can still use it for a guest room." Jan stopped, the familiar sparkle in her eyes. "An old rocking chair would be just perfect to finish it. Oh, Kaye," she gave her a hug, "isn't it exciting? I can hardly wait."

A few days later, Kaye received a call from Jan. "I just read in the paper that a load of antiques has been brought into town from places around Chicago. That antique shop I was in last week has acquired them. They're going on sale Saturday."

"How exciting! Maybe you'll find what you want. I take it, you and Jimmy are going over."

"Jimmy can't go Saturday. He's working on some computer programs that have to be done by Monday. That's why I called. Can you go with me?"

Delighted by the invitation, Kaye agreed, and Saturday morning they drove to the antique shop.

Jan flitted from item to item, oh-ing and ah-ing as she went, with Kaye at her heels. Jan was busy examining an old console model wind-up Victrola and a stack of records when a small chest under a pile of pictures caught Kaye's eye. It was about twelve by fifteen by twenty-four inches, as near as she could tell, with a rounded top. The hinges Kaye thought looked like brass. It was sturdily made with a particularly thick, heavy bottom, she noted. A little work might make it a handsome box for her bureau.

She pulled the chest out and dusted it with tissues from her purse. She worked on the clasp until she finally got it open. Old hinges squeaked as she lifted the lid. The chest was empty. Floral paper, which lined the chest, was faded but its delicate pattern was still clear.

This chest will be just perfect for my genealogy, thought Kaye, once I get it cleaned and refinished.

"Look, Kaye, what I've found!" Jan came toward her with a stereoscope and a straw basket of pictures for it. "I'm taking this now, and they'll hold the Victrola until I can get Jimmy here."

"I've found something, too, Jan. Look!" Kaye showed her the small chest. "Just what I need for *my* genealogy."

They paid for their treasures and went to the car.

When they reached her apartment building, Kaye drove her car into the underground parking. She started toward the elevator with her box in her arms when she suddenly remembered letters in her purse she had neglected to mail.

She got off the elevator at the lobby level and walked out the front door. As she started down the steps to the sidewalk her foot slipped. She grabbed the railing to keep from falling, and the chest she held slipped from her grasp and tumbled down the stairs.

When it hit the sidewalk the bottom cracked and partially separated from the chest. Kaye hurried to examine it. Now she could see why the bottom of the chest was so thick. The chest had a false bottom, a removable board on top of the other, a little space between. The faded paper inside the box covered the upper board. Kaye tried to push the bottom board back into place but something was blocking it. In the space between the boards was a small book.

Kaye carefully withdrew the book. It was well worn but the word "Journal" was still legible. Her hands shaking, Kaye opened the cover carefully and read the printed line, "This book belongs to," and handwritten on the line below, the name "Mollie O'Brien." Obviously added later by a different pen was a second name following O'Brien. The name was "Cook."

Chapter Fifteen

Her heart pounding, Kaye gathered up her things and hurried to her apartment. She dropped her purse on the table, put the chest on the floor, and sat down with the small, fragile volume.

Mollie O'Brien Cook! she kept repeating over and over in her mind. Could this actually be the Cooks who reared William Button? The wife of the Oliver Cook I found in the census records was Mollie, I'm sure. But for this to be her book—impossible!

Carefully she turned the pages and read words written in a childish hand:

"My teacher likes composition very much and she gave me this journal. It's for my graduation from the 8 grade. She said I am to write in here things that are important to me. I guess maybe this is important. Getting out of school I mean. Mama says I should be glad that Papa let me go to school that long. Some people think girls shouldn't go to school at all. Because it doesn't do them any good. I guess i'm glad I can read and write and cipher, but I just like to run in the field and wade in the creek. And eat razberry tarts."

This was followed by a brief description of the ceremonies and her classmates in the little one-room school. Several pages following were filled with anything that popped into the head of what must have been an exuberant teen-ager. Then, like a toy wearied of, there were no entries for a long period of time.

Kaye noted that the entries, when Mollie resumed, were serious. Where Mollie had, at first, mentioned Oliver Cook as a tease and a nuisance, her comments began to show tenderness toward him. Kaye almost felt like an intruder as she read, but she felt she must continue.

"Today I met Caroline Marchant. She just moved to Cross Corners . . ."

There it is, thought Kaye, that little town in Pennsylvania where I found the Cooks before they went to Ohio. I just have to be on the right track. She continued reading, ". . . and she has three of the handsomest brothers! They moved here from Connecticut and took over the Hazelton's farm. I like her. She's such a dear little thing."

Reading the entries, Kaye followed the development of the friendship of the two girls. "Caroline is five years younger than me, and she is just like a little sister. We don't look at all like sisters. She's so blonde and I've got such dark hair. Pa says we look like night and day except for my fair Irish complexion."

With tenderness expected of a bride, Mollie entered an account of her wedding to Oliver Cook and, a year later, of the birth of a baby named Oliver Jr.

Yes, thought Kaye, I remember that from the census. But there still has been no mention of anyone named Button. I don't understand. Maybe they met later or on the way to Ohio. She felt a bit disappointed but she continued to read, entranced.

"Oliver and I went to town today, and we found everybody all upset. War has broken out. South Carolina and some other states withdrew from the United States, and there's fighting. Oh, what a horrible day this is. I just want to cry and cry. Oliver is talking about joining up. I'm so scared."

Kaye read of Oliver's attempt to join the army and his rejection because of a knee injury received some years before. Mollie noted Caroline's distress and pride when all three of her brothers enlisted with Johnny, the youngest, falsifying his age to do so. Almost immediately, the eldest, William, was killed.

Then a strange, intriguing tale began to unfold. Mollie wrote about how Caroline found a Rebel soldier injured in the woods and, confiding only in Mollie, nursed him back to health, then fell in love with him. His name was Alexander Cameron and he came from a plantation somewhere near Richmond, Virginia. He was a confederate scout. Mollie seemed to know little else. She told of the wedding of Caroline and this Rebel at her home, the subsequent estrangement of Caroline from her parents and, later, the birth of a baby named William Alexander.

Oh, now we're getting somewhere, thought Kaye, her fingers trembling with excitement as she read of plans to move to the Ohio Valley. This must be where the Button family comes in.

Then she read a startling entry, "Oh, my dear, dear Caroline! They found her drowned in the creek this morning about two miles from the bridge. Oliver and I guessed that she had made peace with her mother and father, and we thought she had stayed overnight there because of the storm. The horse must have thrown her. They found it running loose. We are staying a day longer for her burying. I'm taking little William with me. I promised Caroline I would take him to Alex. I never thought I would have to keep that promise."

At that, Kaye started. "But his name was Cameron, not Button," she said aloud. "Yet it has to be William Button. But how?" Her heart pounded. She was sure she had found her ancestors. She continued to read.

"That fool, Barney, who shot Alex, has been making a lot of threats all over town. He asked me at the burying if I had Caroline's baby.

"I said no, that he was drowned with her and they didn't find the body. God forgive me for telling an untruth, but Barney suspects that Alex was the Reb he shot back then, and wants to harm 'that spy's kid.'

"Later that day, he saw me with the baby. I couldn't pretend that he was mine because he's so blonde. Anyway, everybody knows Betsy's my youngest. I told him that we were taking him to Pittsburgh to his family.

"He's so mixed up that he believed the story in spite of all the holes in it. He asked who William's family is and I told him their name was Button. It was the only thing I could think of. Caroline always said he was cute as a button. I sure was glad to get to Point Marion and get on our flatboat."

So there it was. Why they retained the name Button in Ohio, rather than his own name of Cameron, she didn't say. Perhaps Kaye would never know.

So my name is Cameron, not Button, she thought. I wonder how Dad is going to take that! Kaye Cameron. Kaye Cameron. Then she spoke the name aloud. It sounded good. She liked it.

There were only a few more entries on the last page in the journal. Kaye read, "We got a letter for Caroline today, forwarded from Cross Corners. We opened it and read that Alex is dead. He was killed in the fighting just three days before Lee signed the surrender. So this is why the letters stopped. Poor little William. Only a few months old and already an orphan. He will never be an orphan, though. I will keep him as my own. As for Caroline and Alex, their life together was brief but the time they did have together was beautiful for them. They would not want to be apart."

Not apart? thought Kaye. But they are apart. Their marriage was only until death. She leaned back in the chair. Suddenly she smiled. But I am the one who can do something about that—and I will! I know now how to make their marriage eternal, how to make William theirs forever. I'll send their names to the temple so they can be sealed. Caroline, Alex and William— sealed forever! Tears of joy filled her eyes as she thought, How wonderous are the ways of the Lord!

Kaye glanced at the clock. She had to tell Jan. She had to share her news or burst! She reached for the phone but it rang before she could pick it up. The caller was Jan.

"Oh, Kaye, have I got news!" Her voice was alive with excitement. "Jimmy came home at noon while we were gone and, on his way back, he picked up the mail and took it with him to read at work. Anyway, he just came home and there was a letter—oh, I've just got to come over. This news is too good to tell on the phone!" The words tumbled out.

"Come right now if you can," Kaye urged. "I've got news, too. Please hurry."

"Look," said Jan, extending a letter to Kaye as she and Jimmy walked in the door. Then, without waiting for Kaye to read it, "It's an old family Bible entry that shows that my Great-grandfather Richard Connors married Betsy Cook! Those Cooks you found in Ohio are my ancestors!"

Kaye looked from the letter to the journal and back again. She was speechless.

Jan continued, "The Connors' were in Monroe County, right next door to Washington County, where you found the Cooks. I'm sure I'll have to do very little more to establish documented proof. We never knew what Grandma Connors' last name was, nor even her first."

Kaye said excitedly, "Please sit down, you two. I've got something to show you that's even better." She handed Jan the book. "Here is a journal kept by Betsy Cook's mother."

For a long time, the three of them read, talked, cried and exulted together over their finds. They now had a bond that tied them together through five generations.

"Of course, we're not really related," said Kaye, "but I feel that we have been drawn together just as surely as Mollie and Caroline were."

Jan agreed. "And when we get the Connors, Cooks, Marchants and Camerons all traced back a few more generations to Connecticut, Virginia or wherever, well—" she shrugged, "who knows what we're going to find?"

"In the meantime, we've got to get these names cleared and sent to the temple. I want Caroline, Alexander and William sealed as soon as possible," said Kaye.

"And the Connors' and Cooks, too," said Jan. "They've been separated far too long."

The first opportunity she had after their conversation, Kaye went to the branch library for the rest of the information she needed to complete the family group sheet for Caroline, Alex and William. She took with her the precious volume. She would give it to Jan, of course, and had told her so. But she wanted copies of the pages that pertained to her own family.

Kaye was marking with slips of paper the pages which she would copy on the photocopier when she had a sudden feeling that someone was watching her. She looked up. Standing not far from the table where she was working were a tall, handsome young man and a smiling young woman, wearing clothing dating, she was sure, to the Civil War. He smiled and pointed to the journal. Kaye looked down at the book and back up at the couple. They were gone. Kaye felt warm and happy. She gave an involuntary little shiver, touched the goose flesh on her arm, and dabbed at her tears. Caroline and Alex wanted what she was doing for them, she was sure. Their faces had expressed their joy.

Kaye wrote to her parents. She told them about finding the journal and what it contained about their ancestors. She was careful not to mention anything that would pertain to the church or its teachings, as her father had ordered. She wondered how they would take the news of the new surname, although, of course, they wouldn't change back now.

The answer came through Kippy.

"Dear Sis," she wrote. "That was fun finding out about the Camerons and Cooks and all. Even Dad showed some interest. I rather like Kippy Cameron. Katherine Cameron sounds elegant! Too bad Dad won't change it. He says I can write to you as long as you don't try to foist your church off on me. You've got me curious, though, and when I'm 18, maybe I'll do a little checking for myself."

Kippy concluded, "Mom sends her love and says maybe you can find out something about her ancestors. Love, Kippy. P.S. We got a letter from Roland and his wife in Denver, and they went with some friends to hear some Mormon missionaries talk. They said they thought it was interesting, and Pop hit the ceiling!"

Kaye smiled. Poor Dad. It would take awhile, but in time . . .

She put the letter on the table and got up to fix dinner. The phone rang and she reached to answer.

"Hello?"

"Hello, Kaye? This is Corey Hollister."

"Yes, Corey. How are you?"

"I'm fine, thanks. The Philadelphia Symphony is coming through St. Louis next Saturday. I have a couple of tickets to the concert they will be playing here. I'd very much like to have you go with me. Would you like to go?"

"Yes, Corey," and Kaye smiled. "Yes, I'd like that—very much."